THE RESEARCHER

The RESEARCHER

A Novella

Lila Samson

Cover and Interior Art by Lila Samson

Second Edition Printing, 2025

ISBN: 979-8-9906103-4-7

In the Second Edition Printing small adjustments have been made. A grammatical error on page 97 had been corrected. Size of the novella has changed from 5.5X8.5 to 5x8.

*To anyone who has looked up at the sky and
found it difficult to look away.*

*Also, to Abby and Arley, my first friends in the
supernatural and spooky – but I want to dedicate a full
book to you both at some point so this only half counts.*

LS 2024

Chapter ONE
fox screams

FOR THE LONGEST time after that heavy, red door swung shut, I just stared at my suitcases. There were so may other things I could have been doing—looking around, putting things in the bathroom, making myself dinner, but no—instead, I dropped them on the warped hardwood, said thank you to Cheryl, the woman who owned the A-frame, and made myself hot cocoa. Then I just I stood in the kitchen, a mug in my hand. Staring. There were only two, it wasn't a huge deal. Just enough clothes for the three weeks I'd decided to stay at this cabin. Yet, unpacking them felt as though I was admitting defeat.

Like I hadn't done that the moment I'd made this reservation.

The worn faux leather slouched with the pressure of my belongings, aching to burst. They looked like they were from the 80's, but every time I laid eyes on them I remembered the first time my mom let me use one. She told me they were my great-grandmother's.

That always confused me.

I took a long, slow sip of my cocoa, licking the whipped cream off my upper lip.

In the silence of the evening, my ears created their own white noise. Whether that was actually something to be concerned with or just my ears refusing to acclimate to the silence of these woods, who could say. Months upon months in the city make people do things—changes the way they sleep, the way they eat, the way they hear. Changed the way I squinted my eyes in incandescents, trying to read the welcome packet Cheryl had left on the kitchen counter for me.

Nights in libraries and study halls lit by hideous, buzzing tubes of mercury were enough to make me need reading glasses after the first year of my doctorate program.

My gaze drifted once more to the bulging suitcases. Through the leather I could make out the sharp shapes of my shoes and the corners of a handful of books that hadn't fit into my backpack.

I hadn't entirely quit the program. The reason I'd rented this cabin for the first month-or-so of the semester wasn't my way of walking out on my doctorate. It wasn't. I just needed...a break.

The old refrigerator clicked and rumbled, cycling through its cooling cycle, shaking me from my trance. In one gulp, the last mouthful of cocoa and cream left the mug, and I dumped it in the sink with an unceremonious *clank.*

The A-frame was split into two levels with the top floor as a sort of lofted bedroom, and the main floor serving as space for everything else. After a failed attempt to lug both Samsonites on the long trek from the front door to the spiral staircase at the other end of the cabin at the same time, it took two journeys up and down the stairs to get everything where it should be.

Honestly, I was grateful the bedroom didn't have a desk. It seems like every place to stay has a desk—hotel rooms, cabins, you name it. And as much as I was not at all running away from my studies, it was nice to have a place where, if I wanted to study, I'd have to make an effort.

Here, there was just good sized queen bed, topped with more pillows than I knew what to do with and the softest quilt I'd ever seen. Beside that, on each side was a nightstand. The nightstands had curved lamps, and one had an alarm clock I unplugged the moment had a free hand.

A single window overlooked the front lawn—well, if you could consider it a lawn. In the fading, evening sunlight, I could still make out the patch of grass, about fifteen feet wide, that separated the front of the cabin from the edge of the woods. There, I'd found a worn spot where the grass was thinner and deader than the rest, and parked my 2002 Toyota Camry.

How that poor creature was still in as good of shape as it was, I'd never know. I never changed the oil on time, and had to nearly shove my foot through the floor if I wanted to brake, but those were the only two issues.

The bed sank when I sat on it. I laid back, spreading out my arms and allowing my eyes to unfocus. Above me, the ceiling turned from distinct wood panels, each knotted and imperfect in their own way, to a blurry brown blob. My eyes creaked with the release. Within moments, they drifted shut.

Silence swirled around me, and soon enough, I fell into the void of half-sleep.

It was there, drifting in that strange plane free from reality and beholden to time only out of kindness, that I finally let my mind go.

A scream echoed outside. My eyes snapped open, my blood ran cold.

Another scream.

I ran a hand down my face, blowing out a breath.

Just a fox. *Dumbass.* Growing up in the city and only spending part of my summers in the woods was enough to teach me what a fox scream sounded like. But apparently it wasn't enough to etch that sound into my mind for all time.

My plan for this trip was to go "old school," like when I'd go on trips with my parents before the internet and the devices that could access it were so pervasive. Disconnect from the world, the media. Isolation may not be my best decision, but it was better than dying.

I'd brought my laptop and phone, but I'd traced my route to the cabin on a physical map and written out turn-by-turn instructions for my drive here. I'd only check my phone one day every week to touch base with family, friends, and the news. My laptop was never to be connected to WiFi, even though Cheryl tried repeatedly to give me the password, and the only things I could use it for were listening to music and watching movies I'd downloaded before leaving the city.

The screen blinked to life and immediately flooded with missed messages.

Others in my PhD program, my professors, and all the way at the bottom, one of the first messages, was my dad, telling me he hopes I have a safe drive and a good vacation.

I smiled at that. He was one of the first ones to tell me to drop out. Not that I planned to, or that I wouldn't go back to my program after this trip, but he was the first one to tell me that if getting my PhD was too taxing on my mental health, he'd rather have a daughter who was a doctorate program dropout than one that hated waking up every day.

My thumbs flew quickly, telling him I made it, telling him to tell mom I love her, don't and forget he promised to pick up the last of my mail before the post office stopped delivering it, "I'll take pictures for you and grab a pine cone," "I love you."

Guilt churned in my gut. Maisie texted me twenty times. After being in the library and the lab together night after night my first year, we'd grown close. It was a weird kind of close. We weren't friends, we never really went out to get drinks or even eat with one another, and most of our texts were in reference to our class or our respective research proposals. Yet we always kept up to date on what we were doing or where we were.

She knew I'd run off.

I shut my phone off and pushed off the bed. The simple act of standing sent pain shooting down my spine.

There had to be somewhere I could stash this...

My eyes landed on a trunk. It was situated off to the side of the towering wardrobe I resigned to eventually stuff with my clothing. It looked old, like it was from the original owners of the A-frame, or perhaps the folks who built it.

My sneakers tapped across the floor. With my fingers still firmly curled around my phone, I knelt before the trunk and opened it.

I wasn't sure what I was expecting. Nothing, honestly. It's a trunk in a rental cabin, if there were anything in it, the most likely contents would be extra quilts and pillows.

Somehow, it was less than that. There weren't any linens, quilts, or pillows stashed within. The bottom was bare un-sealed wood, textured in such a way that held on to any and every bit of dust it could. The only thing in there was an old business card for a moving company based a town away.

I blew out a long, heavy breath.

For some reason raising the hand that clutched my phone took almost all my effort.

But I needed this. I needed to get out.

Screen-down, I shoved my phone into the corner of the trunk and slapped it shut. The latches jingled against one another.

Now I just had to make sure I didn't break my rule early.

The stairs creaked as I went down to the main room, the metal frame solid enough but still digging into the wooden tops all the same. A single lamp lit the room, situated in the corner across from me where the giant far wall, comprised mainly of floor-to-ceiling windows, met the wall covered in picture frames.

It would be a lie to say I wasn't entranced by the shadows it cast. The light was dim, gold—I hadn't been in a room with such relaxing lighting in so long. My eyes ached, but not in the way they did when staring at blue light. It was cozy.

It flickered as the air conditioning kicked on.

For the first time in my memory, I was entirely aware

of the stress lacing my shoulders.

And suddenly, unpacking my groceries in the old 70's fridge and making myself a dinner didn't seem like the end of the world.

Chapter TWO
the silence of space

WITHIN A HALF hour, I'd placed a bowl of ramen (which I'd made fancy with a fried egg, sesame seeds, and a dash of mango hot sauce) and a glass of red wine on the coffee table and opened the backpack I'd thrown on the couch when I'd first arrived. It held most of my books—though these ones were mainly for pleasure, not the classes I was running away from. I pulled out fantasy novels I'd been wanting to read, romances, some cozy novellas, some horror novellas, and then finally, the one that I thought I'd left in my suitcase upstairs. *The Backyard Astronomer's Guide; First Edition.*

A knot tugged in my chest. My fingers ran over the worn cover.

It was my grandpa's copy. He had bought it when it just came out, obsessed with space as he was, and when I was old enough to not be supervised every moment I'd plucked it from the bookshelf in his home office and thumbed through it. As confusing as the big words were to my ten year old mind, the photos were captivating. I got it out every time I visited from then on, and when I had decided on going into an astronomy major, I'd unwrapped that same copy at my high school graduation. His blessing and encouragement, in the form of that book we both loved. Forever off his shelf and on mine.

Holding it now, my stomach sank.

Would he be upset with me? Space was his passion—and it turned into mine. But now...

I put the book aside, opting instead for a short, silly fantasy novel my friend had recommended to me. Between bites of noodles and sips of wine, I found myself giggling, lost in the hijinks of a princess in disguise and her knight friends. The ringing in my ears had faded, and as the night wore on, the sleepy pull of red wine had me slipping further and further down the sofa, pulling a blanket over me, and letting myself slowly wander through the sweet world I'd entered.

After a handful of hours and a full bottle of red wine, I glanced at the microwave clock. The numbers *1:49 AM* glowed bright red in the darkness of the cabin.

I stared at the book. I knew I should get to bed, I knew that...yet I sipped my final glass of wine and turned the page, continuing on.

This was my vacation. I could do whatever I wanted.

Above, the light flickered again. It had been doing that every now and then, as different systems in the cabin turned on and off—the microwave, the kettle, the air conditioning, what have you.

I reached up, tapping the lamp curving over the sofa. It flickered more, growing incredibly dim.

With furrowed brow, I folded the corner in my book

and set it on the coffee table. My cold fingers found the lightbulb and pressed past the burning it set within my skin. I tried to tighten it, tried to loosen it, but it only flickered more. Sitting back on the sofa, I resigned to stare at it. The flickering worsened to a near strobing effect, then cut out entirely.

The whole cabin fell silent.

"Oh, you're joking," I muttered. The clock on the microwave was dark. The air conditioning was silent.

Cheryl did warn me this place could lose power.

Fuck.

Slowly, I rose to my feet. The only light I'd had was that of the lamp—this cabin was too far out in the woods for there to be anything remotely like street lights or light pollution to give me any sort of guidance. What was it she'd said? There was a book on the table with instructions for how to turn the power back on. The box was located in a closet she said...

In my stumbling, I finally found the table and the booklet. Wind rushed by outside, whistling through the cracks in the windows and doors; beneath the pressure, the A-frame creaked.

A line of panic scrambled up my spine.

I wanted this, and now I was alone in a cabin in the woods with my phone upstairs in a trunk and no way to call for help if a masked killer decided to bash through the front door and go all *Scream* on me.

Of course this happened my first night here.

I should have just stayed in school, even if it was making the idea of jerking my wheel in the direction of a large tree dangerously inviting.

The edges of the binder pressed into my hands, my grip tightening as my eyes stretched as wide as they could in a desperate attempt to gather any and all light. Slowly, they adjusted, and I was able to make out the coffee table. Light came in, as dim as it was, from the window wall. Walking closer, the stars above twinkled.

My breath hitched in my throat.

I hadn't seen the Milky Way that clearly with my bare eye in...decades.

Chapter THREE
wind and fire

I HADN'T REALIZED how desperately I needed to see her again until the tears started to burn in my eyes and the back of my throat.

It was gorgeous. A bright, swirling river in the sky, laced with gems of stars, galaxies, supernovas.

The joy, the awe, suddenly shifted.

It was still there, but beside it was grief.

It wasn't fair that something I wanted so horribly, so viscerally, was causing me so much pain. But it *wasn't* her fault. It was the school's, the hoops I had to jump through to be able to work with her for the rest of my life.

The one thing no one tells you about being an astronomer is that you need to take a ton of stupid classes and stress yourself out for four years of undergrad and then five more of a PhD program just so you can get paid to stare at stars and planets all your life. No one tells you it's dominated by men who think they know more than you, even if the topic you're arguing about is what you focused on for your senior year practicum paper. No one tells you that after one year you're going to want to pull your hair out because why should I have to show my work on college level Physics and Calculus courses when I get the right answers and can figure it out in my head anyways?

I swallowed hard.

As much as I booked this cabin in an attempt to get away, I'd also booked it in the hopes that I could reignite my passion for it all.

And now, staring at the stars, the few meteors I see streaking through our atmosphere...my fingers itched for a telescope, for my laptop and my notebooks and my textbooks.

The thought of my textbooks sent nausea through me.

No, no discussion of school. Not now.

Beneath my fingers, the latch on the glass door to the back porch was cold. It clicked a dull, soft click as I opened it, and gave a satisfying *ka-chunk* as I closed it behind me. The porch was wood, made from slabs of pine or something similar. Rain and years of shoes had worn it down to a smooth surface, with only sections that pricked my feet and made me worry about splinters every few steps.

I took a deep breath. All around me was a thick forest of pines, firs, aspens, and birch. Boreal forests had a different smell—they were richer, with undertones of moss and lichen and rotting leaves, even in the height of summer. Now, just as the northern hemisphere began to dip its toes into autumn, the air was cool. A breeze brushed back my hair, my bangs fluttering over my eyebrows before completely flipping up and back in a way that would make me incredibly self conscious on campus.

But here, it's just me and the stars.

A warm wave of peace rippled through me.

The way it's supposed to be.

My arms snaked around my torso, doing their best to hold in my body heat. I should have thought ahead and grabbed a cardigan or a flannel or some sort of warm outer layer instead of just walking outside in the black baby tee and mom jeans I'd driven up in.

Even as chills raced up and down my body, following trails made by the gentle caress of the wind, I didn't mind. I just stared up at the sky.

Constellations started naming themselves in my mind as my gaze drifted. It was always harder with more stars and less light pollution—as a kid, it was nearly impossible to find the images I'd become so familiar with when there were more stars visible than just the ones I'd seen in the constellation guide I'd kept stuffed in my pocket. Now, it was still tough, but I had a good collection I was familiar with.

Pegasus.

Cygnus, my mom's favorite.

Ursa Minor.

Ursa Major.

Vulpecula, I think.

Cassiopea.

I smiled at that last one, that zig-zag of stars depicting that ancient Greek queen. She may not have been a great person, but I still found her constellation comforting. It had been one of my favorites since I was a child. Maybe because it was one of the only constellations amateur astronomers could find that was explicitly a woman.

A meteor shot by.

The Perseids had started a handful of days ago, if I remembered right. The peak wasn't for another few days, so there was a low chance I'd see more than a few this evening.

Still, I let my eyes widen and watched the sky, hoping for another.

There were no chairs on the porch. Cheryl had told me they were all stored in a shed nearby after a large storm had thrown them from the porch, so if I wanted them I had to get them out myself.

I lowered myself to the slatted deck and rested my feet on the steps down, wrapping my arms around my legs.

For a moment, I felt like a child again. Sitting on my grandpa's porch, overlooking his garden, while he pointed at constellations and then found the pages in my kid's astronomy guide that told short stories about the folklore behind them. He was always better at pointing out meteors than I was. Too often I'd get caught up in the current of the galaxy, and when he'd shout out "Look, Bea, a shooting star!" it would already have been too late.

Another meteor tore through the sky and I smiled.

If only being an astronomer were this simple.

He'd be so proud to know I caught more than one all by myself. Sure, I'd spent weeks in a field at night, cataloguing the meteors and their frequency for a class, but I'd always caught less than my classmates. Somehow, they just evaded me.

More wind blew through, tossing my waves into my face and catching on my parted lips. I spit the hair out, pulling it over my shoulder so it could flutter freely, and returned my gaze towards the sky.

One meteor was falling. I smiled, watching the fire build up, watching the bright blue light turn to purple, then pink.

My smile froze.

It didn't break up.

It must have been huge to last that long.

It plummeted closer and closer to the tree line, only growing brighter. Blue and purple trails came off it, coloring the trees, brightening the scene around me—I could see the railings on the porch, the hummingbird feeder, the charcoal grill off in the grass, the shed by the trees that held extra lawn chairs.

My heart started to race. *What do I do?* If this was going to impact nearby, the shockwave could take down trees, it could break windows and set off car alarms, it could cause serious damage.

There was no basement—where was I supposed to go? I certainly couldn't stand outside—if I did, the blast would cause damage to me *directly*.

I scrambled to my feet.

A sharp pain caught in my arch on my right foot—I didn't stop to pull out the splinter though every step was agony.

My hair whipped around my arms, brown tendrils slapping my cheeks, my biceps, my shoulders.

The trees started to bend, leaves tearing free from their branches on the wind, smacking the windows behind me. One sliced my cheek and I lifted a hand, sure it would come away bloodied.

I didn't look at it long enough to find out.

Around me, the world was painted in dark pinks, purples, and blues breaking up the ink wash of midnight.

Every muscle in my body was locked. Every animal instinct within me that was screaming to move got no response from my petrified form.

The ball of fire seared my vision but I did not blink.

Not as it plummeted towards the tree line at terminal velocity.

Chapter FOUR
tinnitus

PAIN RICOCHETED THROUGH my body the moment my tailbone hit the deck. Twinging shocks sparked through me, down my legs, though the entirety of my hips. I couldn't stop the cry I let out, my hands jolting up in front of my face to shield my eyes from whatever could have been flying my way. Light flared through the trees, the resounding *BOOM* rattling the windows of the cabin behind me. I rocked back, my shoulders hitting the glass door—thankfully, neither I or the meteor impact broke any glass.

Every instinct within my body was awake, violent, and terrified. All through my body—shoulders, back, arms, hips, legs—pain vibrated with the residual rumble of the impact.

Heavy, open-mouth gasps fogged the night air around me. My chest heaved—within my ribcage, my heart thundered like a racehorse behind the starting gate.

I needed to call someone. What if that ends up starting a fire, what if that damaged property or—God forbid—killed a camper or hiker?

A dull ringing pulsed in my ears.

My arms shook, fingers twitching, muscles weak, as I pushed myself to my feet.

Another stab of pain from the splinter.

Everything around me glowed a dull, dark purple, the light broken by the shadows of trees. It wasn't close enough that it shone like a spotlight, but pulsing wafts of smoke glowing that same lavender shade were strong enough to spur me into action.

It's so close.

Leaning on the railing, I lifted my foot up, gently feeling for the sliver of wood pricking my arch. Another stab of pain, the ridges in my finger pads caught—I leaned close, squinting to see it in the fading meteoric glow. It was big, but most of it stuck out of my skin.

I pinched it with my nails. One quick tug and a slice of pain freed it from my sole, and a flick discarded it in the grass.

I needed my shoes.

• • •

THE only shoes I had not locked in a suitcase were the ones I'd driven up in: a pair of worn white, platform Pumas with brown and tan leather details. They wobbled over rocks, sticks, and other discarded elements of nature that littered the forest floor. And I, in turn, stumbled like that one bottle of wine was much stronger than it actually was.

Thankfully, aside from the strange, light buzzing in

my head which was exacerbated by the whine that was only just beginning to fade, I felt deeply sober.

The light grew brighter as I walked, using birch trunks and fallen logs for support. The forest itself was dead quiet, with steam and the telltale scent of metal and dirt wafting on a now-hot breeze.

It stung my nose, but I kept walking.

Every step, I cursed myself for not bringing anything to collect samples with. I had no gloves, no knives or tweezers or bags or vials. Only my hands, itching and desperate, and the pockets of my jeans that weren't even deep enough to hold my phone.

This was a *huge* meteor, no doubt about it. That impact was insane, the biggest one I've witnessed. It was nothing on Chelyabinsk—as far as I knew, nothing had been damaged and I hadn't sustained any injuries aside from a bruised tailbone and a sore shoulder—but it was *something*.

And if I could go back to class with this?

I wouldn't be the girl who almost dropped out of the astronomy program. I'd be the girl who came late to school because she got to inspect a meteor impact that happened a stone's throw from her door.

I slipped down a slight hill, catching a branch from a fallen pine to steady my descent.

Well, maybe not a stone's throw. It was at *least* a mile through the woods.

Still.

Branches began to appear twisted, snapped in my direction—away from the impact crater. The air got thicker, the metallic tang on the wind sharper. Slight discoloration appeared on trunks, darkening with each new row of trees.

Charring.

I wrapped my hands around another branch from a fallen birch and swung around a rock, only to have my shoes slip in the loose earth.

The world spun around me, small impacts hitting my head, my arm, my hip, my knee, my elbow, my shoulder. I rolled to a stop, aches radiating from all the points that connected with the earth on my way down. My face pressed into the dirt, hot and sweaty. Gritty, earthy chunks of dirt fitted between my lips—I spat the coagulated dust out, pushing myself up on my elbows. Blinks worked to slowly clear my vision, though my head still spun and pounded. The light was brighter. As I rose, my arms cast pronounced shadows along the dirt. My figure was clear, ringed by a bright, purple, pulsing glow.

Confusion twisted my face.

What kind of comic asteroid had I found? They don't *glow* like that in real life...

Once I gained my footing and cleared most of the dust from my eyes, I spun to peer at the meteor.

Half-buried in the dirt, surrounded by rocks and shattered trees, was a hunk of metal. It was round but angular, with a string of lights pulsing along the sharp edge where two curved pieces of metal met.

I blinked at it. This had to be a hallucination, the side-effect of a mental break I didn't know I was suffering.

But there it was. So obvious, so cartoonishly obvious a child could have cited the proper name, and even known exactly where the little green man should be sitting.

Chapter FIVE
sounds of terror

THE WORLD AROUND me slowed. Smoke rising in a steady plume drifted in slow motion. Then, I laughed.

I laughed loud and long, my throat hurting, my eyes burning. Some strange primal fear woke within me, snaking through every muscle in my body, begging me to move, to run. I had no idea what was concealed within this craft or what it would do with me.

Yet I dropped to my knees, panicked, awestruck tears streaming down my cheeks.

"No fucking way," I managed. The laughter had taken hold of me, visceral and inhuman. My eyes roamed the shape ahead of me, repeating again, at the top of my lungs, "No *fucking WAY!*"

Hair, matted and dirty and quickly being weighed down further with a build up of sweat, hung in my eyes as my shoulders curved in. My hands hit the hot dirt to support me. In the earth, my fingers curled into fists.

Laughter subsiding, I heaved breath after breath. "This is... insane."

There had been theories, of course—most of the others in my classes agreed that there had to be *some* sort of life on planets, but most of us assumed it was plant life, or bacterial, or something altogether unidentifiable as life to us earthlings.

And yet...

Son of a bitch, *why don't I have my phone?*

The worst of my panic began to subside. Dusty hands wiped over my cheeks, smearing dirt into my lashes.

Pushing myself up, my entire body felt numb. The earth I stood on was disturbed and shifting as it was, but that coupled with my jelly legs made for a very wobbly walk towards the craft.

A dull *thud* rang out through the trees when my hands hit it.

"Holy shit," I breathed.

I wasn't going to be the girl who almost dropped out of her astronomy program, and I wasn't going to be the girl who witnessed a meteor crash—

No, I got to open discussion about the existence of extraterrestrials.

And I got to do it with *proof.*

The metal was smooth beneath my palms, issuing that same static fuzz that you'd get running your hand over an old TV. Every movement, every touch along the surface sent rich purple ripples over the silver. It was only covered in soot, not burned. The slightest pressure was enough to wipe the blackening from it. Parts of it were dented, others torn to bits. Small pieces of alien shrapnel had embedded themselves in the dirt, the trees it took out with its fall.

And it was *cool*. Despite the fact that it was just falling sixty-two miles through the atmosphere at terminal velocity, burning up with the pressure and friction of just entering our atmosphere, the metal wasn't hot. The earth was hot, the steam was hot, but the metal was so cold I wanted to press my face to it like I used to do with the tiles in my childhood home.

The craft creaked and I skirted back, stumbling over rocks.

If it was opening, if it was moving, who knew what would be inside it?

Who knew what would get *out* of it?

Fighting through the pain lacing my bones, I scrambled back up the side of the crater, latching on to a few branches jutting out from the bottom of a huge pine tree and flattening my back against it best I could.

My heart raced.

After a moment, I heard the earth shift. The craft groaned again, followed by dull thumping. It was repetitive, like someone knocking on a door or—

Or trying to kick open a stuck door.

The *clang* of metal giving way echoed through the trees, followed by a thud of something heavy hitting the earth.

Strange, warbling, looping tones wove through the trees. My eyelids grew heavy, my head spinning at the sound. It was that awful, disorienting feeling I got after waking up from an unexpected afternoon nap.

I clenched my jaw together and let my eyes shut, doing my best to not make any sound as the calls struck at the most primal parts of my mind.

I wanted to run, I wanted to scream, I wanted to curl into a ball and cry.

Finally, the sounds subsided. My body slowly felt like my own again, and when I got enough courage, I took a deep breath.

I shifted as slowly, quietly as I could. This thing was from an entirely different planet—most likely an entirely different *galaxy*. To say that it could have advanced hearing or sight or smell was an understatement.

It might have senses entirely nonexistent on earth.

I peeked out from behind the tree, my eyes landing on the craft. There was a panel open—the door itself laid in the dirt a good five feet away. But I saw nothing else.

Get up, that primitive part of my brain screamed, *get up, run, get away, get AWAY*.

And yet, I couldn't help but sit there and stare.

I wasn't an engineer. I didn't study astrophysics much, only the little information I needed to start mapping stars and understanding how galaxies formed, the transfer of matter through space, and so forth.

But I couldn't help it—I drank up every detail of the craft. I needed to know how it ran, where it came from, what it was made of, what kind of propulsion it used in atmospheres and in the vacuum.

My thoughts stilled, however, when my eyes landed on small, purple shapes embedded in the earth.

They weren't there before. I would have noticed.

Swallowing hard, I stood, inching out from behind the tree.

Whatever the alien piloting the craft was, it wasn't here. It likely couldn't see me.

Again, that's assuming it sees in a way even remotely similar to the way we do.

Slowly, I positioned my feet on the edge of the crater sideways, so I could slide down the side the way kids slide in their socks on hardwood. I'd go, grab one of those glowing things, a sliver of metal if I could, and book it back up to the forest floor and back to the cabin.

A heavy breath huffed from my nose.

Three.

Two.

One.

I launched myself down the loose dirt. It skittered beneath my feet, much louder and way bumpier than I'd expected. A few timed I'd stutter step, making sure I didn't tumble on my face.

Within the craft, those haunting, tones echoed.

Fuck.

My shoes hit solid ground. I ran. I bent over. My hand closed around a glowing purple shard of crystal.

The sounds grew louder, combined with clattering within the ship.

I stood. I ran to the edge of the crater, tugging a shard of metal out from a tree—it folded in my grasp like paper.

That's it. That's all. GO.

More rocks clattered free as I climbed, sliding down and twinkling against the craft and the bits of it that had detached for one reason or another.

Something exited the ship.

FUCK.

I crested the top of the impact crater and ran. No rocks stopped me—my shoes slipped, nearly breaking my ankle, but I kept going. My lungs burned, my eyes hurt to keep open.

Those *sounds* got louder.

I'd never run this long before. My heart thundered in my chest, forcing adrenaline through my veins.

The A-frame appeared.

The steps rattled as I ran up, the door making a horrible sucking sound as I wrenched it open, breaking the storm seal.

It slammed shut.

I locked it.

I didn't stay there. A quick survey of the cabin led me to dive behind the end of the sofa. I clutched the crystal and the crumpled metal to my chest, my breaths coming in fast, panicked gasps.

Time stretched strangely.

Every sound sent a jump along my skin. The things in my hands thrummed with their strange energy. The house creaked against the wind, and I bit my lip, waiting for the door or a window to break. Waiting for whatever made those awful sounds to find me.

Whether it was an hour or five, I sat there. I focused on my breathing. I did my best to curl my body around the glowing things I'd stolen.

Then, the microwave beeped, and the lamp turned back on.

Chapter SIX
the snap of a polaroid camera

DAYLIGHT BROUGHT ONLY a modicum of peace. After the lights went on, I'd stayed there for a handful of minutes before stuffing the crystal into my pocket and the metal under my shirt. Then, I took a deep breath and sprinted to the lamp, turned it off, and pressed my face against the glass, staring out at the darkness.

It took too long for my eyes to adjust, but when they did, it was just as empty as it had been when I was watching the Perseids. With a heartbeat so loud my hears throbbed, I brushed my hands off on my jeans and went upstairs.

The loft bedroom had a single chair in it, near the stairs. It was large, comfortable—the kind of recliners you'd see at your grandparents' house, with a soft maroon fabric that pilled in areas. I dragged it to the window that overlooked the back of the house. Then, I pulled the samples from my pockets and placed them in the trunk, right next to my phone and that journal.

Then I sat in that chair by the window until the sun came up.

With each moment, the sky lightened. My head nodded, and when I lifted it up with a snore, the sun nearly blinded me.

I could have cried. I'd never been so happy to see him.

It meant I could see. Every movement in the trees, every stretch of silence where the birds stopped singing, it all gave me an edge up on whatever was going on.

On whatever could be out there.

Rubbing my eyes only served to irritate them—my hands were still covered in dirt, my face sticky with dried sweat.

A hot shower remedied that.

During school, whenever I was stuck on a project or an assignment or even a simple concept I couldn't wrap my head around, I'd always turn the water on—near scalding—and stand beneath it, letting the flow wash away my muddied thoughts until they came up clear and bright.

Even when I took a shower without that intent, it happened.

So, as I was lathering lavender and peppermint shampoo into my matted, dirtied tresses, my mind began to wander.

Daytime means I have an advantage, being a diurnal creature native to this planet. I could very well revisit the crash site and take pictures, catalog things properly, and gather more samples. Even if I didn't choose to revisit it today, I should do what I can to analyze the samples. I don't have a full lab, and I'm not a geologist—usually we'd let those guys analyze any meteoric samples we'd get in, and then we'd just interpret the data, but as things turned out, I'd have to be a one-woman research lab.

I tilted my head back and closed my eyes, washing out the soap. I could see myself in my mind's eye, pacing before a blackboard and writing out a list the way I usually did prior to tackling a big project.

Okay. Here's what you're going to do.
1) You're going to get paper. You brought notebooks, get them out. Use them. You need proof of this.
2) Record every starting observation you can about the metal and the crystals.
3) Figure out basic tests to run—easy things like conductivity, weight, that kind of stuff.
4) Get pictures of the crash site.

I frowned at that last one. It was best to go back. Not just for me, not just to get a little speck of comfort from seeing the alien craft in the sunlight, but for the sake of greater scientific advancement. If I could get good, clear pictures of the crash, if I could run *tests* at the site—

A large crash of water fell from my hair as I squeezed it too quickly, too harshly.

No, I couldn't run tests at the site on my first visit back. I didn't know what I was getting into.

The water turned off with a harsh squeak from the faucet.

I needed a weapon, too.

Shrugging into clean clothes, I tied my hair back in a braid and dug my scuffed boots from one of the old Samsonite cases.

5)   Unpack your damn clothes.

One thing I'd made sure to bring in an attempt to further my cellphone detox was a proper Polaroid camera. I'd not had one as a kid, but when they started becoming popular again, I snagged one and stocked up on a ton of film. There was always something about pictures taken on a polaroid. They felt more...real. Maybe it was due to the fact that it was harder to edit a hoax into that kind of a medium.

I slipped it around my neck, took a deep breath, and stared out at the woods from behind my glass door.

There was absolutely nothing out there. Not that I saw, anyway. There was still a crash site only a mile from me, with a likely hostile creature prowling around it. Desperate.

At least, I assumed it's desperate.

I would be, if I were in its shoes.

The lock clicked as I turned it. The door made that same sucking sound when it opened. All around me were the subtle, calm chirps of birds. Leaves brushed one another in a soft whisper, matching the soothing brush of wind on my cheeks.

Everything was fine.

Closing the door behind me, I brushed my bangs off my forehead, only for them to flop right back into place. For a moment, I got the image of myself standing on the deck clearly, as if I'd teleported a few feet up and to the side of where I stood. My eyes were sunken from lack of sleep, my lips cracked from the constant licking—a nervous tic I'd done since I was a kid. Exam seasons were always awful because of it. My dark, wavy, shaggy hair flicked out of my braid in sections, amplifying how crazed I felt.

I blew out a sputtering breath.

This was *so* stupid.

The deck shook as I walked across it. Absently, my fingers found the camera hanging around my neck, the tote bag I'd slung over my shoulder and filled with a notebook, pen, and an a single knife from the kitchen.

It likely wouldn't do anything, but it made me feel better to have.

Unlike the evening before, which was cool and already beginning to herald the transition into fall, the worked hard to draw out the moisture from the plants and make everything beneath the canopy humid and stuffy.

To keep my mind from spiraling, I counted my steps. It was twenty before I got to a downed log. Then I counted again. Another downed tree. Restart. 24. Downed tree. Restart. 17. Restart. 14. Restart. 10. Restart. 5. Restart. Restart. Restart.

My heart hitched each time that number got smaller. I knew what it meant. I knew I was getting closer to the impact. And when I could hardly take a step without having to dodge a log or balance from one trunk to another, my hands started shaking.

Leaning on the same pine tree I'd hidden behind the night before, I gazed into the crater.

It was huge. I'd not noticed last night, it was too dark and there was too much going on. But it easily stretched twenty five feet in diameter, maybe more. The craft itself had a central line of about ten feet. In the daylight, it really was just an equilateral triangle with domed faces. The door was still kicked off, the inside of the craft dark save for a handful of random blinking lights in various shades of purple, blue, and red.

I sat there for a long time, watching the lights blink. A few had turned off—maybe the bulbs burnt out? Or broke? If that's even how they worked.

But most importantly, the site was silent. The only movement was the lights along the edges of the craft, flickering in a round.

I took the camera in my hands, crept out from behind the tree, and lifted it to my eye. There, in the viewfinder, was the best picture I could take.

Click.

My lungs stopped working as the picture whirred out from the bottom of the camera. Blood thudded in my ears, washing out the crinkling of the flapping polaroid. I waved it through the air a few times before stuffing it in my bag. The camera hit my stomach and I scrambled down the slope, catching myself before my feet tripped over one another and sent me tumbling into the crater yet again.

It wasn't that tall. Maybe it was the fear from last night, but the size of the ship wasn't that impressive when lit straight on with bright, golden sun.

I snapped a few more pictures: the dirt it embedded itself in, the door, the metal shrapnel around it, the lights...

Wait.

I squinted, stepping closer than I would have if my common sense had been working at that moment.

Brushing over them lightly, my fingertips caught on stiff, pointed objects. They flared when I did, but I pushed back the panic building in my stomach.

A rush flew through me as I tapped it again, and it responded with that same flare of lavender light.

I found the knife in my bag quickly enough, fitted the tip of the blade in the minuscule space between the light and the metal body of the ship, and flicked my wrist. On the first try, the knife just scraped against the light and flung out haphazardly. I stumbled back, breathing hard.

If this fucking alien doesn't wake up and kill me, who knows, I may impale myself.

My neck cracked as I rolled it in an attempt to hype myself up and force back the dizziness swirling at the corners of my consciousness. I placed the knife back in the same spot and forced it to go deeper, using my other hand to wiggle the light out. The thing flickered again, more erratically this time. But again the blade slipped out. It missed my left thumb by a hair's breadth.

"One more time, Beatrice, one more time," I breathed. My words caught in my throat, the whisper coming out squeaky and hoarse.

I shoved the knife in. It caught.

Gritting my teeth, I dug my short, cracked nails into the gap on the top and bottom of the light and wiggled with all my might.

A scratch echoed, and it dropped out into my waiting hand.

I dropped my head with a heavy exhale.

There, in my palm, rested a long purple crystal, not unlike the one I'd snagged from the dirt the night before. I rolled it back and forth, the cool crystalline texture reminding me of the quartz towers my sister put around our shared bedroom in high school.

There was comfort in it.

That comfort faded the longer I stared at it. The longer I studied the way it shimmered, the way it produced its own light, the stranger I felt. Shivers crawled up my arms, my back. Fingerlike twitches stretched up the back of my neck and cradled the bottom of my skull. Every vein in my body seemed to try to arch towards it.

With a sharp blink, I shoved it in my bag. A strange tingling still radiated from my palm—I did my best to rub it off on my jeans, and when the sensation didn't fade, I picked up my camera again, and snapped a few more photos, regardless of the fact that I'd taken the same ones moments before.

Chapter SEVEN
the buzz of electricity

THE TWO CRYSTALS and sheet of metal just sat on the table, unmoving. I wasn't entirely sure what to do with them. After coming back from the crash site, I'd pulled out my notebook and the things I'd stuffed in that trunk, placing them all at the center of the table with the new crystal I'd removed from the ship that morning. Then, I'd poured myself a glass of water, sat down, and stared.

Part of me expected them to do something all on their own.

They were alien, after all. Maybe they themselves were a form of life.

But no. They just sat there. And I stared at them, and they stared at me.

Shadows shifted on the floor as the sun drifted above the cabin. I drank my water and fought the urge to pick them up again. That weird tingling sensation still buzzed within the bones in the center of my palm, and as much as I ached to take those strange rocks up and run tests, comparing the one that I removed from the one I picked out of the dirt, it didn't entirely feel like my own desire. So I pushed it down, crunched on the ice left in my glass, and lifted the metal up to my face.

Normally, I wouldn't be the one running tests on this, and if I was, I'd be recording my observations on my phone.

My eyes fixed on a space in the middle distance, a blurry speck of dirt on the floorboards.

I could go get my phone. This was *huge*, and it would be completely understandable for me to stop my technology detox to record what's happened.

But I've already taken polaroids and laid them out on the table beside me. I have a clean notebook I can use for all my findings. I can make this legitimate. And so I refocused on the metal, took a deep breath, and bent it.

It was so strange. I'd remembered it being flimsy, like paper or tin foil, but seeing the sheet of metal fold under the slightest pressure was jarring. And the moment it was no longer under pressure, it would spring back into shape.

I made a note of it.

For a moment, the thought of putting it in the microwave crossed my mind, but if this was anything like aluminum foil, I'd risk burning down the cabin with that. Perhaps the whole forest. So instead, I pulled a lighter from my backpack and held it underneath until my fingers burned. The metal gathered soot, but like at the crash site I could wipe it clean with the slightest touch. And the other side was cool, almost to the point of being cold, as if there was absolutely no heat transfer at all.

Picking up the pen again, I scribbled down my notes.

Does not transfer heat.
Melting/burning/charring point unknown.

After trying to poke a whole through it, which turned out to be impossible, and trying to fold it in a way where it would keep the shape without using outside tools to keep it in that shape (which *also* was impossible), I set the scrap of metal aside and chewed my lip.

I have to figure out what's up with these stupid fucking crystals, whether I want to or not.

One stayed pinched between the first three fingers on each of my hands. Just looking, it was clear which one I'd removed this morning and which one I'd taken last night. Aside from the light scuffing on the side of one, the light it produced was stronger and more vibrant in shade than the other. Held in my left hand was the one I'd plucked from the dirt—when I'd initially grabbed it, the crystal looked like a purple quartz point. Now, it was nearly colorless, with a vague shimmering purple energy radiating through it as I rolled it in my fingers.

In my left hand was the new one. Its glow was brighter, the natural stone itself a brighter shade of purple that rippled with the energy I felt pulse down my fingers.

It was... fascinating. Weird. I hated the odd, tingling rhythm it sent through my bones, but I couldn't bring myself to put it down now that I'd picked it up.

If I had wires, I could make a circuit. Test if there is any inherent electricity in it, or if this was a different kind of energy source than any we're familiar with on earth. My mind darted back to the old alarm clock I'd unplugged and left on my bedside. There had to be a way to create a makeshift circuit with that, right?

The crystals dropped onto the table, rolling a little with their own weight and velocity. Before I could realize what I was doing, I had gathered up a screwdriver from the small toolbox Cheryl had left for me and dragged my alarm clock down to the first floor.

I wasn't going to destroy it. That would make too much of a mess and there was a great chance that Cheryl would make me pay for it. So, instead, I cracked off the mechanical carapace and exposed the innards, selecting a few wires and removing them ever so carefully.

Without being plugged in, the clock would not work. It was useless to try the circuit without an energy source. If I plugged it into the wall and stuck the crystal between two specific wires, however....

Kneeling by the wall, I plugged the alarm clock in. Nothing happened, seeing as I'd ripped out part of the circuit. But I rolled the pale crystal in my palm and flopped onto my butt, sitting criss cross and bending over the experiment with my whole body. It was like I'd been thrown back to the after school science club I'd joined in fourth grade. Twice a week, after hours of learning and listening, I chose to walk out to the "temporary building" that stayed there even after I'd left for college and sit on the floor, just like this, with a weird little contraption in front of me. Then, I was asked to figure out how it worked. Most of the time, I got halfway there but ended up confusing myself somehow, and then our instructor would sit us all down and make us watch an educational video or listen to her short lecture before doing it again.

A smile crossed my face at the notion. I'd always missed it, even in college. Sure, I was studying astronomy with the big dogs at that point, but there was something so simple and inviting about hunching over a cobbled together experiment to learn how the world worked.

As I fit the crystal into the slot I'd created, my smile faded. The wires had not yet been fully connected, but it already began to buzz with a current, sparking and glowing all throughout the structure of this strange, foreign mineral.

I leaned closer, tapping it with my finger.

Nothing transferred. Not even a dull pulse, like with the other one. The screen began to flicker its characteristic *12:00* to show that the power had been disconnected. I tapped the other wire into place on the opposite end of the crystal, and the glow within it became brighter. White sparks began to leap from side to side, end to end.

My heart pounded.

It was beautiful, and yet I couldn't shake the fear that one of those was about to arc off and light the cabin on fire.

In a bout of panic, I snatched the crystal out of the circuit.

It was still, somehow, cold.

My teeth buried into my lower lip. Between two fingers, I raised the crystal up to my face. "You are so strange," I mused.

Remnants of electricity sparkled and crackled inside it. After having it in close contact with my skin for a longer period of time than tapping it, a faded buzz began to transfer. Like waving your hand over an old TV, where the static would jump out to meet you and leave that strange metallic smell on your fingers.

I pushed myself from the ground, the crystal and the

alarm clock tucked safely in my arms. My back ached after bending over, but fell right back into that passive ache born solely from stress and exhaustion once I sat at the table again.

There was nothing I could do to bring myself to grab that other one. If the one that held less of its initial charge still ricocheted the energy within it and sparked that much, what would the other one do?

Still holding the crystal, I held it up before my face. White dots danced around within it, the last remaining traces of the electricity. That slight buzz passed through my fingers. With my right hand free, I found a pen and scribbled down my observations.

CRYSTALS:

Lesser-Charged One

- *Does not transfer heat*
- *Transfers electricity*
- *Holds a charge*

And then I stared at it. I'd specified the "Lesser Charged One" out of habit. Out of the ingrained action of differentiating test subjects, recording every variable. Even though it implied I would be testing the other one.

My eye fell on the second. The stronger one, with the scuffed side and the glow.

There were still other tests I could do that didn't involve touching it much.

Chapter EIGHT
the thrum of blood

THE TONGS WEREN'T the best choice, but they stabilized it enough. I'd placed the crystal on a rock outside, the flattest one I could find, then grabbed my sunglasses, tongs from the tool rack beside the fireplace, and a hammer from the closet. Cheryl had some of the weirdest things here, like that random journal upstairs and a hammer in the closet right beside a box of rusted sewing supplies and a bear trap, but I wasn't mad. One of those things came in handy, who's to say the rest wouldn't, either?

The late September sun glinted off it even though it was unpolished. I absently pushed my sunglasses further up my nose. It was the best form of eye protection I could manage at the moment.

I raised the hammer, straightening my left arm best I could to ensure proper distance from the crystal should all shards fly.

A knife had scratched it.

A hammer *should* shatter it.

Swinging it down, I closed my eyes.

A *crack* echoed through the forest not unlike the crunching of glass. A sharp pain tore through my left forearm—I jumped back, dropping the tongs, the crystal, the hammer. Blood dripped down to my palm in a thin stream. I tore my sunglasses off and threw them aside— whether they hit a rock or dirt, I didn't care. Every movement sent pain shooting up my arm to my shoulder, down to my fingers. I twitched as I stared, trying to lift my arm close enough to my eyes to peer into the half-inch laceration, hesitant to poke it should I voluntarily shove the agent that did the cutting deeper into my skin.

My vision faded as I turned and found my way back up the steps to the cabin.

Oof, I've never reacted to blood like this. I shook my head, steadying myself on my ascent to the deck. *It's just the shock. Not actual shock, but the shock of this even happening. Am I breathing okay?*

The door creaked open. It shut behind me.

Through my fogged vision, I zeroed in on the sink.

"Wash it out," I mumbled to myself.

The room swirled with each step. My eyelids had become full of lead, blinking slowly and erratically.

It wasn't the blood. I never reacted to any wound like this, not even when my brother cut off his finger in the kitchen. It was that stupid piece of crystal. I could feel it. It was there, in my skin, pulsing, shooting off whatever strange electricity it carried.

My fingers, dumb and groping, found the faucet—a *whoosh* of water flooded my senses and I kept my eyes open long enough to angle the wound just to the side of the stream. Too much pressure from the water would cause it to push the shard further in. Too little, and it wouldn't wash the blood away, and I'd have a hell of a time trying to get remove the foreign object now embedded in my muscle.

The water was cold. It was almost a shock to my system, forcing my eyes open. They strained in my skull.

Beneath the flow of tap water, I realized I wasn't overreacting moments ago. I could feel it. Every shift, I felt the sharp mineral scrape along the inside of my arm. Shocks of electricity coursed through my veins.

My chest ached with the frantic slamming of my heart against my lungs.

I need to get it out. Now.

The first thing I thought of was Epsom Salt. It was the only trick my babcia ever used, unless the thing was so big she could pick it out with two of her long, always manicured finger nails.

But I couldn't use that in an open wound. It would cause too much of an issue, dry out the tissue and refuse to let it heal properly.

My mother's go-to was always tweezers.

Which were upstairs in my suitcase, alongside dirty makeup cases.

Not sanitary, but it was necessary.

Tearing off a wad of paper towels, I pressed it to the wound just enough to dry the water and catch any blood still seeping from it. With a deep breath and wobbly steps, I climbed the stairs.

It was darker up in the loft. I'd noticed that the first time I'd stepped up here, but now it was even more so. Thankfully, my bag still sat exactly where I left it, propped against the dresser, my makeup bag sticking out of it.

With one hand I unzipped it and turned it over, dumping the contents onto the floor.

Sparks shot across my vision.

My brow furrowed.

There was no way the charge held in the single shard I'd managed to hurt myself with was strong enough to send those kind of signals through my whole body.

I blinked it away. That was a problem for another time.

My mission now was made of one single goal.

It gelt like my eyebrows were digging into my hairline, trying to scrape my hair back further, dig into my forehead, my skull itself.

The tweezers trembled. No, that was my hand holding the tweezers. I did my best to spread open the mouth of the wound by forming a fist and craning my hand back, but it didn't do much.

With a deep breath, I dipped the tweezers closer.

Just like playing Operation.

Pain rolled through my body with each vague pass of the tweezers. I could almost hear it—the metal scraping against that rough chunk of crystal, already thinking it's part of my body.

Gone were the electrical currents. Every feeling came in waves. Heat. Pain. Cold. Fear.

Tears welled in my eyes. The tweezers, the blood, the glow within my arm—it all blurred together in a watercolor of viscera and fear.

I closed the tweezers one more time, fully ready to accept that I may just have to call Cheryl and have her drive me to whatever the nearest hospital was and get it surgically removed—but I felt that *crunch* you get when pressing rock a little too hard on concrete.

I pulled.

Instantly, the pressure in my body lifted.

Blinking away tears, I saw it—there, pinched between the two ends of the tweezer, was a tiny shard of crystal, dripping with my blood, pulsing with latent energy.

It wasn't more than half the size of my pinky. Not particularly small, but not particularly big either. Considering the size of the one I'd broken it off from.

I threw it in the trash. There was nothing else I could use it for, and as the adrenaline cycled through my blood, I found myself glancing at my bed repeatedly.

It was comfortable. I was thankful for that.

The quilt was soft beneath my fingers. It was warm when I slept in it last night, and after everything that had happened I'd rationalized it as a bit of a safety blanket.

Still, I pushed away and made my way down the stairs to properly clean and bandage my arm.

Every step was heavy. My bones had been laced with liquid metal, sloshing around at each move, desperately trying to throw me off my feet.

At least that pulsing was gone. At least the electric current that had been using my veins as a highway wasn't there anymore.

Once I'd placed a few bandages over the cut, I let myself flop down on the sofa. Outside, I could still clearly see the rock I'd used as an anvil, the sparkling, shimmering remains of the crystal, the tongs, and the hammer. And to the side, half-covered by uncut grass, sat my sunglasses. No part of me wanted to get up. Every voice in my head said I needed to—that's what adults do, we make messes and then we clean them up.

But my head dropped back, nestling perfectly in the

cushioned back of the sofa.
My eyes fluttered closed.

Chapter NINE
white noise

STARS EXPANDED OUT around me. For a moment I couldn't tell if I was floating or walking on something. Nothing but the vast vacuum of space extended below me. I watched as stars blinked into existence, and as others blew themselves out in catastrophic supernovas, birthing nebulas and black holes alike.

It was amazing.

Galaxies swirled around my arms, above my head. Twin stars danced through the air in their spiral way.

One floated by my face, shimmering and twinkling. The star was only the size of a housefly. Leaning closer, I could see the arcs of flares and the lapping, rippling flames that made up the body of the red giant.

My breath caught in my throat, nervous that if I exhaled, I could accidentally blow it off course or entirely extinguish it.

I lifted a finger. The heat coming off of it was kin to

touching a light on a Christmas tree.

"Don't mind her," a voice chimed.

I startled, stumbling back—well, wobbling back. The empty array of space caught me in an invisible hold. It was strange, my body felt like I was swimming, but I never sank further than where I was, and when I lowered my feet, it somehow felt like I was standing on something.

A rippling laugh echoed. "Careful now! Don't want to take out a galaxy now, do we?"

No one was there. The voice was loud, echoing—as if the owner of it was right next to me. Yet I spun in place, my hair drifting around me, my clothes lifting and rippling with whatever invisible force held me up. "Hello?"

My voice hardly echoed.

"Hello!" It responded.

The stars twinkled with the syllables.

I furrowed my brow, anxiety starting to push out the awe I'd felt. "Who are you?"

"No, I'm supposed to ask that about you."

Out of the corner of my eye, a shimmering figure appeared. It was human-shaped, but was entirely made of coalesced stars, planets, and galaxies.

"You're...where are you from?"

I blinked. "Earth?"

"Oh!" They snapped their star-fingers, a strange grin spreading across what they tried to make their head. "That explains it!"

"Explains what?"

"Why you look like that. Tell me," they took slow steps towards me, and with each inch closer, the stars grew thicker, filling out the visage of a human woman's face that blended in to a construction of constellations for a body. She smiled. "Why did you take the crystals? You weren't stealing them to sell, I hope."

My breath hitched, eyes roaming her face.

She was beautiful. Anyone would acknowledge that. A woman made from stardust—from stars themselves—was more awe-inspiring and stunning than anyone on earth.

Yet so close, I could see how her form was a mere approximation of a person. She had no true understanding of humanity. Her smile splayed too wide, her eyes made of manipulated nebula remained unblinking. A dull roar emanated from her, as though the vacuum of space originated within her chest, holding her being together.

Being near her was like white noise.

I blinked. My heart beat an uneven pace, thrown off by the uncanniness of it all. "Sorry,what? Where am I? This..." I spun around, dragging a hand through my hair as I studied the setting. "This is a dream, right?"

My eyes settled back on her face, and it took everything in me not to jolt back as she pressed closer, her nose almost touching mine.

"I don't know. You Earth-children have strange relationships with the subconscious."

A hard swallow worked its way down my throat. "Um..."

Her eyebrows lifted. "Yes?"

"Can you take a step back?"

At this, she did blink. Once, quickly, a flash of shifting matter and darkening of stars. Then, she laughed, gliding back. "I've never met one of you before! You're so interesting, what, do you need such a great emptiness between you and your friends?"

Questions muddled my head. If this wasn't *really* a dream, what was happening? And what was she, who was she? What does she mean she's never *met* any of us before?

"No," I stuttered, forcing my way through the strangely calm form of panic roiling around in my head. "We have what's called personal space, you can get close just..." I waved my arms to create a bubble, "not any closer than here."

"Hm," she mused. When she moved it was more like swimming than walking. She pushed off of whatever strange surface we stood on and floated sideways, staying at the same distance from me as she circled around me. Wisps of starlight trailed from her feet as she kicked them back and forth, comets dancing at the ends of her hair. "So what are you? You don't look like the kind of creatures I usually find."

My mind wandered. This *had* to be a dream. Yes. It had to be. I fell asleep after...after digging that crystal out. After a long night of a lot of strange things.

She asked you a question, Bea.

"Oh," I shook my head. "Sorry, what did you ask?"

"What *are* you?" She repeated.

"Human," I answered.

"No, no, I know that," she waved her hand, floating to a stop on the other side of me. "I mean...I've seen your satellites. The...what was it, the record you sent out? All the other calls for attention, too." There was that laugh again. "You humans are some of the noisiest ones out here. If not *the* noisiest. So are you a...what did they call it, 'cosmonaut?'"

The word sounded strange coming from her tongue.

The letters thick, harsh.

"That's the Russian term. Astronaut is the American one."

Her eyebrows raised. "Okay? Does that matter to me?"

A good question. "I...uh..."

She laughed again, flipping backwards like mermaids do in kid's cartoons. "But seriously, what are you? A scientist? A musician?"

"I'm an astronomer," I said. When she didn't answer, I fiddled my fingers. "It's someone who studies space."

"A researcher!" She chimed.

I nodded.

"Oh, good. I do love working with researchers. What questions do you have?" At this, she suddenly sat down before me, legs crossed. That smile was softer now, not nearly as inhuman as it should have been.

I sat down too.

After all the things I'd wanted to know—about the spacecraft, about the crystals, about her—my mind emptied. Every thought eddied out into the cosmos around me, pulled at by the same vacuum that held me.

After a moment, she blinked again. The second time in the entirety of our meeting. "I'm offering you knowledge, Researcher. I'm serious. I don't usually get to have an even give and take with someone. I'm...excited about this. Ask me anything."

When I didn't answer, her brows furrowed.

"Do you not want to learn?"

"No," I stuttered. "I...I do I just think...I'm a little confused." Uneasiness flooded me, but as soon as she smiled again, it ebbed back out into a sea of emotion.

Her eyes sparkled. "That's okay, we can work through

that together! This has been something I've wanted to do for centuries!"

My mouth dried at that. "Centuries?"

She nodded dramatically, hair of nebulous clouds and shooting stars floating around her head. "I'm a traveler. Like that little friend," she raised a glowing finger and pointed at a passing comet. "Except I can't do things on my own. I'm only here because the last person who helped me crashed into your planet." That grin split again, and she leaned forward. "And then, you found me! It's okay, I'm not so much like you all that I can't handle being broken into pieces, but it is easier if I'm put together. Or of there's more of me."

I shook my head. Everything was getting confusing. Painful, almost. A deep pressure began to squeeze my temples, the roaring emptiness from within her sort-of-body becoming nearly deafening. As she continued to speak, I saw her lips moving but all I heard was that roar.

"I'm sorry," I interrupted, a hand up. "I can't hear you, it's so...loud."

A third blink, and with it, her eyes relaxed. No longer were they wide, crazed. They seemed deeply earnest. The hum of space faded to a soft whisper. It wove its way between us, carrying a single lilted "sorry." Her voice caressed the pained areas in my mind. I could nearly feel a hand brushing my cheek with each curling syllable. "I didn't mean to dump so much on you. I just...I get excited to meet new people."

She stood, starlight-woven gown spilling past her knees and onto the floor, chunks of space swishing with every movement as though it really was fabric.

In a few paces, she stood before me and knelt down. "Maybe we should try this again another night."

The dream began to peel away at the edges, separating from whatever shell it had attached to. Space rippled, stars broke off and plummeted past me, down, down, down into nothing.

Any part of me that would have been worried jumped to full panic. My heart raced, my head hurt. My lungs ached with each speeding breath. Every blink, more stars fell from the sky.

The cosmos was *melting*.

"It's alright, Researcher," she cooed, that too-large grin back on her face. "I'll be here to talk when you're ready."

Chapter TEN
the closing of a trunk

I SAT BOLT upright, drenched in a cold sweat. Through the large windows, orange late-rays of sun cast dancing shadows through the rest of the cabin.

My eyes shut involuntarily, and I tipped my head back once more.

What a weird dream.

How long I'd been out, I wasn't sure. But the way the whole living room glowed was enough to tell me I'd slept for a good few hours. When I went to move, my body was heavy, lethargic—it took all my energy just to throw my weight forward to stand. Dull aches ran down my arms. I trailed after them with light, simple touches, as if I could brush them away. Nothing worked. My fingers only brushed over the bandage on my forearm and then my skin. But the dull, throbbing ache remained.

A hand ran through my hair, ruffling away the bangs that flopped right back onto my forehead.

My eyes fell on the makeshift laboratory at the table, the bloodied paper towels by the sink, and finally, the hazardous mess I'd left outside.

Time to be an adult, I suppose.

It took me no time to clean up the alarm clock and the other crystal. The clock, along with my notebook, photos, the scraps of metal, and all the pens and other random things I'd piled at the table for my experiment got placed on the steps up to the bedroom—the way my mom used to pile my things when she'd be cleaning and not want to deal with my crap laying around. It always got me to bring it to my room, so I'd kept the habit. Pocketing the faint crystal that still held those small sparks bouncing back and forth within its faceted face, I swept the towels into the trash and wiped up any bloody droplets that I'd missed on the white Corian countertops.

Armed with a plastic Ziploc and a tiny hand-broom, it was finally time to march outside.

A fresh wind blew. I could hardly smell the smoke from the impact anymore. It was cold and bright and thick with the sweet decay of leaves. My toes wiggled against the cracking porch, and for just a moment, I let myself close my eyes.

This was still my vacation.

Opening them, I carefully stepped towards the rock and the brutal murder I'd committed atop it.

Bag open, broom sweeping, I clenched my jaw.

This is still my vacation.

This crash was stupid and distracting, but someone from the government had to show up and get rid of it eventually. That was something in all alien movies—the Men in Black appear out of nowhere, and suddenly it's like the crash never existed.

If they did exist and if they did come here, it would be for the best if I didn't have any connection to it when the time comes.

Yet, in the back of my mind, I couldn't help hear my inner voice chattering with a million questions.

Where did it come from?

What are these crystals?

Who was that in my dream?

What does the alien pilot look like, can they even survive in our atmosphere?

How did that spaceship fly?

And the most childish of all: *what constellations do they know that I don't?*

That was something I'd always thought about. The constellations we see from earth are specific, we're so far from them they look like they don't change because it takes so long for any movement to become recordable for us due to how light travels. But say you're south of where we are—relatively, since space has no direction—and look up. Orion would be entirely different. Cassiopea may look more like Cygnus, or something entirely new.

What was that like?

I zipped the shards—and small, nearly-powder piles —into the bag. It looked like I'd crushed candy, or an amethyst. The weird glow had all but dispersed. Now it was just small sections of mineral formations, easily confusable with any number of things from our world.

The top of the Ziploc wrinkled in my curled fingers. Within, the shards twinkled against each other, sounding more like glass than the strange quartz-adjacent material they actually were.

The moment the door closed behind me, a knock pounded on the door in front of me.

My heart leapt into my throat.

For some reason, even though I knew it wasn't the alien pilot—they probably don't even have a concept of knocking before entering—a sick wave of fear twisted my gut.

"Beatrice? It's Cheryl, are you alright?"

The anxiety churning my insides didn't let up. I took a deep breath, pocketing the crystals and snagging my flannel off the back of a kitchen chair. It would be easier to face her if I didn't look to have anything strange on me, and if my bandage was covered.

Buttoning the middle one, I strode towards the door. "Cheryl?" I called, just before opening it.

The woman stood there, curly greying hair tucked into a claw clip. Her hands were shoved into the pockets of her sweatshirt. "Beatrice!" She repeated my name, eyes wide. "Are you alright?"

I furrowed my brow. "Yeah? Why, did something happen?"

She blinked at me twice in quick succession. "Did you not hear the meteor crash?"

My heart raced. "Oh, yeah, I did. Nothing was damaged here though, I'm fine, the cabin is fine."

Nothing has been cleaned up. You still have everything out on the table. She'll see it and question it and then it'll get taken away before you have a chance to learn anything.

A quick glance over my shoulder confirmed that the panicked voice in my head was wrong. I stepped to the side. "Do you want to come in? I can put on some coffee. Since you drove all the way here."

At this, one hand left the pocket in her grey *Duluth, MN* sweatshirt and batted at the air. "No, no, it's fine. I was heading in to town and figured I should stop by and see if you were okay. It shook *my* house last night so I was a little worried about what it might have done to the cabin. Or you, if you'd gone outside."

I forced a smile. "No, I just stayed in. Watched it from the windows. One of the first things we learned when beginning to handle materials from crashes like that is the simple fact that we don't know what could be on them. We're familiar with our own world's bacteria and parasites, but we don't know if there are any off-world that could come to us through meteors or what have you. Or if we'd even recognize them as such when they do." The laugh I gave was genuine. "I'm not stupid enough to open myself up to possible inter-space parasites."

She glanced behind me, then back up to me. A smile graced her face, and after a moment, she laughed too. "You've got a good point."

For all her nervousness, it was clear she believed me.

She had no reason not to, I realized. Up until last night, I'd just been a burnt out grad student looking for an escape. I'd told her about my program, what my dissertation was on, what I'd wanted to do for my capstone next year. I'd told her about my family and how my aunt used to have a place nearby I visited as a kid and that's why I wanted to come back up here.

"Well," she scanned the forest behind her, all a swaying rainbow of leaves. "Are you enjoying it here so far?"

Warmth flooded my chest, and for the first time all day, my shoulders drooped. I nodded. "Immensely. It's peaceful and beautiful and...I am truly having a good time."

That smile broadened, and she backed down the steps. "Good to hear. Well, I've got things to take care of, so I'll leave you to your evening. Have a good one—and if you need anything, you know how to reach me!"

I smiled back. "Of course. I'll check in with you later!"

As her sneakers hit gravel and crunched towards the waiting white truck on the drive, I backed up, ready to close the door.

She hopped into the driver's seat, started the engine, and tossed me a wave.

I lifted my arm to wave back, pain shooting down my forearm. A grimace twisted my face. I quickly covered it with what I hoped was a convincing smile.

Once she starting backing down the gravel road, I closed the door. Every trace of panic flooded out of me, and with it, a bolt of sanity came to my mind.

What the fuck was I doing?

I'd rented this place out to escape space, to escape my field, to recover mentally before diving back in, and so far the only things I've done to aid that initial goal were drink some hot cocoa, wine, and read. Then the meteor crashed and every plan I had for relaxing went to shit.

A deep sigh flushed out of my chest. Resolve settled where my frantic curiosity had been writhing moments earlier.

Without a word, I collected the things I'd left on the steps and trailed my way up to the loft. Dappled sunlight danced across my bed. The warm tones of the quilt glowed with a welcome heat.

The trunk in the corner of the room caught my eye again.

I dug the crystal from my pocket, as well as the bag with the shattered one, and tossed them in very unceremoniously. They were soon followed by the shrapnel, the alarm clock, and my notebook.

The lid closed with a heavy *thunk*, and I lugged over my suitcase. It rested on top, open, and with a breeze floating through the windows I'd forgotten to close, I finally unpacked my clothes.

Chapter ELEVEN
a gentle voice

I WAS GOING to have a good vacation.

With a freshly poured glass of wine, some chicken sizzling on the stove, and a pot of noodles boiling, I sat atop the table and simply breathed. Slow inhales, steady exhales. I took in the rich, earthy scent of my wine, the lingering undertones of pine that still managed to stick to the wood panels lining the walls and floor.

My sweater was soft—I'd forgotten I'd packed it. After two days of wearing the same jeans and black baby-tee, I'd finally traded in my duds for something more relaxed. Comfortable.

If I were a writer, I'd say it was the perfect author-in-a-cabin outfit. An oversized Aran sweater, courtesy of my girlfriend from freshman year, and loose flannel pants patterned with the least-specific plaid ever—green and black, with the occasional string of red running through. Swirling my wine in my glass, I glanced back at the stack of books I'd unloaded and placed on the coffee table. On top of the pile (mainly comprised of fantasy books) sat two shitty romance novels I'd been gifted by my sister when I'd fully moved away for my PhD.

"Since you're gonna be too busy to get any," she'd said, her blue eyes glinting as I unwrapped the old mass market paperbacks.

"Shitty" was perhaps not the right word to describe them. I'd not opened them, just judged them by their covers, and isn't that one of the cardinal sins of reading, even though everyone does it?

They had the usual designs—a dramatic woman with long, luscious hair and a gown that was practically falling off her chest, clinging to a man with an eight pack and no shirt.

It wasn't the worst option for the night. I was supposed to be having fun, connecting with what made me human, right? As much as I wasn't the type to get lost in sex scenes clouded in purple prose, maybe that was the right choice for tonight.

All in all, I couldn't think of anything less related to the cosmos than the Scotsman and his accidental bride on the cover of the topmost novel.

It would provide a good distraction. Even if all I did was giggle at the writing and the entire lack of plot.

Tearing my gaze away, I stirred the chicken. It had marinated in the cream sauce I'd prepared long enough. I drained the noodles, ladled them into one of the low-sided bowls Cheryl had stocked the place with—or a "plowl" as Maisie and I called them—and topped it with the cream sauce and chicken.

Soon, I lounged on the couch, sipping my wine, eating bites of decadent dinner, and thumbing through the pages of *The Highlander's Lady* with a grin on my face.

The night turned darker than it was, and by nine, I'd finished bottle of wine I had left nearly-empty the night before. I flew through the book—I didn't so much read it as skim the pages, laughing at the descriptions and grimacing at the lack of autonomy given to the leading lady.

Somehow, halfway through my second bottle of red wine, I'd wandered onto the porch once more, and stared up at the sky.

It swirled now. The thick swath of stars and galaxies spinning even more through clouds and that dark evening tapestry made me dizzy.

My butt hit the wooden boards, and I laid back, letting myself twist and twine with the cosmos itself.

I've had too much to drink.

The dark outline of my hand scattered some of the light as I raised it up, tracing out the few constellations I could see.

The night sky was so simple. So beautiful. I loved charting paths of comets and marking down every incremental shift in the orbit of a satellite at the edge of our solar system. I loved it because it meant I got to understand this great, breathing ecosystem of which humanity was a part.

I loved it because it meant I got to stare at the sky.

"Fuck the aliens," I muttered. "Fuck the UFO, fuck all that." A smile crept across my face. "This is what matters."

My vision split and fractured with uneven blinks. I could have floated off the earth and into space and not noticed, the way everything began to swim around me.

Tiny pinpricks of warmth scattered across my skin as the specs of stars drifted down to kiss my cheeks, my arms, my collarbone. Unbidden, my eyes fluttered shut. The tiny spots of warmth grew, sweeping across my brow, my shoulders, down my back. I shuddered.

The silence of night faded into a dull hum.

Even the wood slats of the deck supporting my limp body were warm, fading into the soft void of night.

"Researcher," a voice whispered.

Chapter TWELVE
the warped tick of a melting clock

MY EYES SNAPPED open.

Her face hovered inches from mine, grinning down at me with that same too-wide smile.

I gasped sharply, sending a chunk of dust straight down my throat—it scraped along the soft tissue as I swallowed and then immediately began trying to hack it up.

The Traveler's eyebrows crunched together, forming a bright spot of galaxies between them. Her smile stayed fixed.

My hands hit whatever invisible boundary was beneath me, staring into the deep expanse of space through watery eyes, each breath bringing with it more pain. My throat was raw—more than it was from inhaling whatever star I had vacuumed up,

Her face appeared beneath me, still that strange mix of excitement and concern.

I threw myself back as she rose past whatever boundary was keeping me up. Frantic hands swiped at the tears still clouding my vision. "What do you want?"

My tone was short, pained. I didn't want to talk to her—she was...interesting. The way those nebulous eyes followed me, the way those galaxy-lips stretched. But this was a dream. A dream I didn't ask for a sequel of. In fact, it was a dream I'd explicitly tried to forget.

"Leave me alone, I don't want to talk to you."

Her expression fell. "What? Researcher, I thought we were friends."

Doing my best to quiet the animal within me that was begging me to run as much as it was begging me to reach out and touch her, I gritted my teeth. The grinding sound they made was painful. "I'm done with this. I don't want to have this dream anymore, wc can be done."

Waves of long, comet-tail hair floated up around her as she shook her head with frantic, fearful movements. "No. No, please, I...I just wanted to talk to you. I thought we'd agreed to do that. To share knowledge."

I stood up, and so did she, mimicking my movements with her closest approximation of human behavior.

Internally, I cursed myself. Every time my mind turned towards a mode of escape—forcing myself into lucidity, trying to conjure a clock and read time—that white noise emanating from her silenced my thoughts and I found myself lost in the swirl of stars.

"What are you?" I asked. "Really, not just a traveler. What are you?"

Her smile returned, hesitant. "I'm a traveler. That's all I am."

"What is your purpose? What was your homeworld?"
God, Bea, shut up. Just get out of here.

The thought was gone before I could acknowledge it.

She blinked, long lashes scattering stardust with the movement. "Sit, I'll tell you." A single, gentle hand pressed on my shoulder until I stumbled back just enough to let the back of my heels connect with the armchair that suddenly appeared behind me.

Slowly, I sat. It seemed real. As much as anything here could seem real. The leather was cool beneath my palms. It was smooth, too. I ran my fingers over the seam on the armrest, tapping along the brass nails holding it together.

A matching one, red leather with brass nails, appeared behind her. She sat and crossed her legs, the movement scattering stars from the hem of the strange, shifting, gown-like garment she wore.

"I am from a world far outside yours," she started with a grin. "My kind are travelers, I would never lie about that. We go from planet to planet, multiplying and scattering. Learning. We mean no harm. We merely want knowledge. I merely want knowledge." Her grin stretched wider, once again tipping into that uncanny appearance that sends chills down any sane human's spine, and even some of the insane ones. "I cannot tell you how much I want to learn. There are so many planets, so many stars—I want to see them all. So you can imagine how excited I get when I meet a kindred spirit."

My teeth gritted against each other. How could I know anything she said was real? "Are you a spirit?"

This *had* to be a dream.

Clock. I need a clock.

Her head bobbed back and forth. "I'm not entirely familiar with that word, but if I had to answer I'd say yes. Of a sort. To your kind, at least."

The steady *tick, tick, tick* of an analog wall clock began to thrum through the space.

"So this *is* a dream," I muttered. Turning in my seat, I only caught a glimpse of her as the smile faded, making way for a swirling, furious mass, with pits where those glowing planetary eyes had once been. My eyes landed on the clock, its numbers already starting to melt, and then I turned back, adrenaline spiking as I fully registered the image I'd seen.

There she sat, though. As still and wondrous as usual. "Why did you ask for a clock?"

"So I...could check the time," I said. It was a lie, and she knew it. I could tell by the way a single brow momentarily flitted upward.

"I do not mean to keep you, Researcher," she said. The now-warm leather beneath me disappeared the vacuum of space once more cradling my bent body. "I'm just...excited, I suppose. It's not every day I get to have an equal exchange with someone."

"Uh huh," I craned my head back around, but the clock had already begun to fracture into the cosmos.

"I've seen so many constellations from light years away," she mused, her voice soft as silk. That gaze that was on me moments ago drifted over the scenery around us. "And I've always been one of the only ones to see them. I'd like to share them with someone else."

I glanced over at her.

If there was any doubt about it before, I knew now: this was absolutely a dream. Nothing that happened here mattered, it's all made up by my subconscious as my body recovers from the day.

And I'd been so tired.

Pain streaked through my left forearm and I glanced

down, expecting to see that shard of crystal protruding.

In the dream, though, my forearm was bare. Free of any scratch, any cut—even the bandage was gone.

"There are so many distant plants and galaxies I've seen and just...well, it's hard keeping it to myself," she giggled.

My eyes rose to her again.

She held my gaze. Suddenly, she seemed much closer than before. Every bit of her was mesmerizing. I hadn't let myself get lost in someone's eyes for far too long.

The longer time I spend here, the longer I sleep, I realized. *Might as well give in.*

I leaned in, studying the soft confines of her face, the way stars twinkled in her eyes when she noticed my close attention.

She smiled. "I can see it in you. You want to devour meteor showers like I do. Experience diamond rain. Walk through sand as smooth as silk. Watch stars you never even knew of blink in and out of existence." Her hand slid over mind, suddenly solid and burning.

I didn't move away.

"Imagine what we could learn together, Researcher."

"My name is Beatrice," I said. I didn't know why, but the way her whole face glowed with an even wider smile was enough to keep me from taking it back.

"Ask me, Beatrice," she purred, "and I'll show you more of the universe than you could ever hope for."

Her hum was deafening, a roar that drowned out all my thoughts but one.

I swallowed hard. "Show me."

Chapter THIRTEEN
voices when there shouldn't be

SHARP DISCOMFORT SHATTERED the strange sleep I'd fallen into. My brain throbbed within my skull. If I was back at my program, living in that tiny apartment near campus, I absolutely would have assumed it was a symptom of drinking too much the night before. But the sun was cutting through my eyelids, piercing and golden and brighter than I'd ever remembered, and the only thing I could taste was the stale remainder of a 2022 Malbec.

The deck creaked beneath me as I rolled to the side. Greasy hair swung into place as a sweaty, stiff curtain, shading my face from the outside world.

That's what you get for drinking wine and falling asleep staring at the sky instead of in your cozy, safe bed, Bea. A weird dream and a pounding headache.

I pushed myself up, pain streaking through my left arm. A quick glance confirmed it was bleeding again. The dark crimson had begun to seep through the gauze—it wasn't a lot, but the bandage was shifted enough that I cursed myself for not being smarter. As a kid, I'd been no stranger to picking at scabs or moving my wraps and bandaids in the absolute wrong way so I ended up tearing off the scab that had begun to form.

My nails scraped against my scalp, sending shivers down my spine. It felt so good to loosen that horrific tangle I'd somehow created. Blood rushed to my head as I stood. Beneath me, my legs were no more trustworthy than jello.

In a pitiful stumble towards the door, I found it wavering in the morning breeze, slightly ajar. It swung open with little more than a nudge. Leaves that had blown in overnight crunched beneath my bare feet on my path to the kitchen.

A normal morning routine included starting my morning with with coffee or tea, maybe a hot chocolate if I wasn't feeling the caffeine, but this morning the fridge clicked open and within moments the snap and hiss of a soda can opening echoed through the living room. The sweet, crisp bubbles did little to wash away the bitter aftertaste of the wine, but it was enough to make my own mouth bearable.

Back against the sink, I scanned the room. Nothing had shifted. My book was still open butterfly-style on the coffee table, beside it the open bottle of wine.

The door clicked open again. I frowned. Soda in hand, I marched over and shoved my hip against it. The glass rattled in the pane, but it did, finally, lock.

My entire body felt gross. Like dirt had curved into every single part of my body that was not a plain expanse of skin on my chest, my arms, or legs. The leaves crunched as I scooped them up and tossed them in the trash.

It may not be as clean as my apartment, but it's close enough. For now.

After draining the soda and tossing it towards the trashcan—which I missed—I ignored the voice of my mother in the back of my head telling me to wipe it up before it dried and became atrociously sticky and a breeding ground for ants, and instead gathered the single scented candle Cheryl had placed on top of the refrigerator and trekked to the bathroom.

Just the steam on my skin was enough to make me claw myself out of my clothes. The water rushed behind me as I worked out the leaves and tangles that had knotted my hair overnight. With everything I needed hung on the back of the door and every garment I'd discarded in a pile near the sink, I stepped under the rushing water and closed my eyes.

It slid over me, burning. Eyes closed, I let myself focus on the heat, the way it felt like it was stripping my skin clean.

Then, I unwound my wrap.

It was better to clean it in the shower and bandage it after, I'd figured. The soap and the constant stream of water would do good to clean it.

Blood-crusted gauze stuck to my skin, pulling and making me wince. Every layer I peeled away brought another, even more soaked with blood.

These bandages were wound too tightly. Only when I started unwinding them did I feel the blood fully returning to my fingers, hot and pulsing and strangely itchy.

Stars clouded my vision at the sensation. I blinked

them away, stumbling back, catching myself on the slick shower wall.

"Easy, darling," a voice purred in my ear.

In one move, my feet slid out from beneath me, my hip cracking against the side of the bathtub and pain shooting up my back as my tailbone slammed against the floor.

A long, pained moan echoed through the bathroom, breaking up the rhythmic pattering of the water still pouring out of the shower. The unceasing stream hit my shoulders and chest, splashes covering my face in tiny droplets.

I opened my mouth to breathe, and coughed at the water I inhaled.

Everything hurt.

My nails curled into the ceramic sides of the tub in futility, one hand taking a fistful of shower curtain as if that would help.

On my feet again, I slowly checked my body.

The start of a bruise was already forming on my left hip, right where the bone stuck out, with one mole my mom always had said she would use to identify me if I were abducted.

Other than that, I was in one piece.

My gaze trailed down my arms, checking for any other bruises, cuts, or what have you I could have suffered...

I stopped.

The bandage covering my wound was gone, I'd taken it completely off, and it had been soaked with blood.

Right?

A quick glance to the pile of gauze sitting in the soap tray confirmed yes, that indeed was true.

I ran my thumb over the place in my forearm where the cut should have been.

Should have been.

The soft pads of my fingers only brushed a thick, pale scab. An older one. Not the brown of a fresh scab, only a few hours old, but the pale one that had been replaced day after day, until only a little bit of the wound was left to heal.

Absently, I scratched at it. The scab stuck to my forearm, nearly half the length of my pinky and so solid I couldn't get my nail under it, but as they ran over it, a deep, electric itch burned down my arm.

I flattened my palm against it and rubbed.

Mom always said when nails made it worse, non-specific pressure helps.

The wound was hard. Whatever scar tissue had formed...

No, there was no way it had healed already. It was a day. A full day. That's it.

Holding my arm up to my face, I peered at it intently. Only a day, right?

A single blink felt like my eyelids were dragging across my eyes, suctioned to the sclera.

No matter. The scab was a scab, the would would heal on its own in whatever time it needs.

I shook my head, stepping carefully to reposition myself and indulging in a lengthy, hot shower with multiple shampoo cycles.

An hour later, wet hair up in a bun, I donned my Aran sweater once more and a pair of running shorts. I'd intended to clean up, but in the silence that comes with no music, no television, no traffic, neighbors, or even roommates, everything felt so strange.

Romance book in hand, I climbed the stairs to my room and tossed it unceremoniously onto the bed. Small as the paperback was, it jumped along the quilt before flinging itself off the edge in a comical manner.

I walked over to that side of the bed and bent down to grab it. Everything swam as I shifted—that happened when I was younger. The overwhelming buzz was familiar to me. Each snap of darkness pulling at the corners of my vision, each swirl through my head.

A flat palm pressed against the cool, polished wood beside the book.

I closed my eyes, breathing steadily.

When they opened, the sun was already starting to dip below the tree line.

My stomach growled, but I ignored it and trotted downstairs to slip on my Pumas. The way the wind rustled through the trees was so inviting, and as I stepped outside, I found my gaze drawn towards that section of the woods I'd been lost in a handful of nights prior.

I wanted to go back. I hated to admit it, but I couldn't stop thinking about everything I was missing. Everything I could learn.

No.

This was a *vacation.*

I bounced down the steps, my hair swishing behind me, sticking to the wool and dampening it.

This was a vacation, and I was going to immerse myself in the woods like I should have been since I first got here.

The chilled early-evening air nipped at my legs. Back at school in the city, I would have immediately turned around and thrown on sweats. I hated any sort of discomfort, my PhD program was giving me enough to last a lifetime. It had gotten to the point where I would go to my labs in a pair of sweatpants with the ankles cut so it hung loose and a grey tank top I'd had since high school.

Yet I closed my eyes and flexed my fingers in the chilled breeze.

Discomfort was good here. The cold wasn't going to kill me, I didn't have a project due that required my utmost focus.

Maisie would have been so excited I was finally taking time to be in the present. She was all about mindfulness.

With the night air filling my lungs, I finally started to understand why.

Sticks and the leaves that had begun to drop more by the day crunched beneath each step. My hands wobbled out to the sides, catching branches and trunks to steady myself until I finally felt sure in my footing and let myself jump around.

After a few minutes of exertion, I paused to catch my breath. My cheeks hurt from the constant smile I'd discovered plastered there. But like everything else this evening, it was good.

I'd drank water. I'd showered. I'd done absolutely nothing of importance all day.

My meandering path continued until my shin connected with a fallen tree.

My stomach twisted.

I didn't need to be back here. I didn't even plan to walk in a straight line—I was jumping everywhere, swinging from branches and trees...in a way, I'd expected to be lost. Not...

Stop it. I closed my eyes. *This isn't a big deal. You're not going to be...doing anything. Just looking.*

But a look was all I needed to break my vacation again. I knew it.

My feet moved forward.

Within my chest, my heart jumped, stuttering the rest of my body to a stop. I hadn't approved the movement. I hadn't let myself go.

I had just gone.

"You'll be fine, Bea." I exhaled, raised my shoe, and planted it on the other side of another fallen log.

Before long, the trees thinned.

Ahead of me, I saw...

The crater.

Just the crater.

Chapter FOURTEEN
silence. again.

IT WAS SOME sort of...cosmic blessing. Yes. That's it. The universe knew how this would stop me from recovering, and resting so it just...made it disappear.

I stared into the empty crater, mouth agape, unblinking.

This is good, I told myself.

This is good.

Rocks clattered against sticks and each other as I slid into the impact site.

This is good.

My hands pressed to the divot—no, the *pit*—in the earth where just days ago there had been a UFO. There was no evidence left of it. No metal, no burns, no crystals. Just the hole it had once inhabited.

This is...

"What happened?" The whisper drifted silently from my lips. Nothing ever just disappears, that's the cardinal law of matter. Mass cannot be destroyed it can only be dispersed. *Matter* cannot be truly destroyed. There was a ship here, and now there's...

I stood up, dusting my hands off on my pants. Fists clenched and unclenched by my sides. Within my chest, my heart hammered faster than it ever had. My face felt... fuzzy.

This was not my problem.

Not anymore.

Slow steps took me backwards, away from the crater. Even the dirt had been smoothed over, as though someone had taken a huge rake through it like they do on baseball fields between innings.

No crystals poked from the earth. A gash ran through the trunk of a tree, but the metal that had made it was long gone.

But it wasn't my problem.

My arms hurt as I climbed out of the pit.

I did not jump or climb as I walked home. My gaze remained fixed on the path just a few feet ahead of me, arms swinging stiff and straight at my sides. When I climbed the steps, my knees cracked with the unnatural movement of it all. In the kitchen, I grabbed a pot and filled it so I could make...something.

I had some potatoes left, if I'd remembered right. I could make mashed potatoes. And...chicken nuggets. Maybe. If I brought them. I think I brought them.

My hair nearly dripped into the water as I stared at it. At the tiny little bubbles forming along the flat steel bottom. At the reflection of myself that seemed so unlike myself.

Everything was the same, that wasn't the issue. My eyes were distant. I didn't even realize I was staring at myself until I blinked and saw the subtle movement reflected across the gently rippling surface.

Try as I might, my mind kept wandering back to that empty crash site.

The sound of a knife skinning and chopping potatoes faded into the background, the repetitive action becoming automatic.

I knew who it was.

That craft didn't just disappear, it was taken.

The potatoes plopped into the water. I brushed the boiling droplets off my hand, but the pain didn't fully register.

They didn't find me though. They didn't yet know I was a part of all this. Wasn't that what the Men in Black did? Erased memories, covered alien sightings?

Or was that just in the movies?

I think I would realize missing time or strange memories.

My nails tapped a frantic pace on the counter, finally shoving me off into a pace around the room.

This wasn't good. It couldn't be. The options were awful: either the Men in Black were real and took the ship, or some local stumbled upon it and...also took it? I guess?

Chewing on my bottom lip, a third possibility came to mind.

I could have imagined it.

It made sense. I'd been burnt out when I came here, only a few days after my therapist had reminded me that I tended to throw myself headlong into things without considering my health. She'd been proud of me for taking time out. She'd told me she didn't want me thinking about my dissertation or anything related to my program for the few weeks I was here. It had almost broken me, almost killed me.

And what was the first thing I did?

I went and stared at the sky.

After everything, I must have just...snapped.

The dreams and the Traveler were easily explained by a mental break. Hell, even the UFO crash was. It *was* a meteor, and the ship never was there, and over time the meteor just...burned itself away? Or maybe it hadn't even landed in the first place, maybe it was a ghost-impact of sorts.

Was that even a thing? I couldn't be sure anymore.

My eyes fell to my arm, and the small cut on it.

I *had* gotten a cut. But had I just...broken a *normal* rock? Had something *else* cut me?

Before I knew it, I was climbing the stairs to the loft. A single light illuminated my room—one lamp beside the bed whose dimmer switch I'd turned all the way down. During my time in the woods, the sun had already managed to dip behind the treeline and begin the sky's inevitable sink into darkness.

There was no time to turn on a light. My knees slammed against the wood.

I felt like I was going to throw up.

Shaking fingers wrapped around my suitcase, pulling it off the top of the trunk. The latches undid with a snap.

Maybe it was better to just assume everything was a psychosis. Maybe I should just call my therapist, or Maisie, or my sister, or my parents.

But then again, my phone was in that trunk too.

So I'd have to open it anyway.

Swallowing hard, I lifted the lid.

There, placed exactly where I'd left them, was a baggie of crystal shards, the one in-tact point, a stack of polaroid photos, and my phone.

Somehow, it didn't make me feel better.

So the crystals were real. That means the ship was real too, which means it *did* just, somehow, disappear.

I slammed the lid shut before I could do anything else.

Then, after a moment, I opened it again and dug everything out. My notes, the specimens, everything.

Even my phone.

It was dead. Of course it was, who was I to ever expect it to work after a handful of days turned off and in the back of a trunk.

After a full ten minutes of digging through all the bags I'd brought, I finally plugged it in. The little charging symbol flashed, and I belly-flopped beside it and the other items I'd tossed onto the bed. The crystal bounced with the movement, one of them rolling to press against my right arm.

The moment it made contact, what had originally been a buzz turned more into a wave. Not a constant electric pulse, but a steady crescendo and decrescendo of energy.

Before I could move to push it away, a warm breath swirled by my ear. "Come on, Beatrice."

My entire body went still at the voice.

"You *know* you can't fight that. Not when it's as... welcoming as it is."

Every inch of me flooded with adrenaline.

She was *here*.

No, she couldn't be, she was in my head.

But I know that voice.

Part of me wanted to try to respond with my face pressed into the mattress the way it was.

The other part of me knew this protocol from when she was scared of ghosts as a child. Waking up in the middle of the night, fearing something was in the corner of her room.

Don't move, don't breathe. If you pretend you're sleeping and slowly open an eye to look, it's safer.

It'd be even better if you didn't look, but I was an adult now.

Adults had to look.

I slowly counted down, pulse rising, until my entire body was running cold with adrenaline and fear.

Then, I looked.

Chapter FIFTEEN
cracked, strange speech

THE ROOM WAS empty. The breath I exhaled was long, forceful. I sat up, crawling towards the headboard, blood still thundering through my ears and the cold swirl of nausea rippling through my stomach.

It was empty.

Maybe not all of it was a breakdown, but part of this *had* to be.

I swept the notebook and crystals into the drawer in the bedside table. As my pulse faded from my ears, it was replaced with the sharp hiss of water on a gas burner. Racing down the stairs, I found nothing more than a mostly-evaporated pot of water and burnt potatoes.

The bottom of the pot was blackened.

I dumped the whole thing, potatoes and all, into the sink, started filling it with cold water, and slumped against the table.

Tears began to prick at my throat.

This trip, which was meant to help me recover and unwind, has done nothing but prove to me that I am incapable of being normal. Everything is over the top. Everything is all or nothing.

Even insane, stupid hallucinations.

I burned a *pot*. The only time I did that was when I was a kid and didn't realize I'd left the burner on after making mac 'n' cheese for the first time. And I can't remember the last time I didn't wake up from sleep utterly exhausted and pained. Every moment felt like I was slogging through muck, especially after waking up on the porch this morning.

Swallowing hard, I dug through the fridge before I found the least-bruised apple in the bunch.

This was good enough for dinner.

. . .

A strange, pin-pricking feeling trailed down my bicep. Even half asleep, I swatted at it. Habit from the summer months when leaving a window open too late into the day meant mosquitos had found their way inside. I'd still seen them buzzing about when I'd gone into the woods.

Snuggling deeper into my blankets, I hoped I'd killed it.

Ow.

I flinched, swatting at my shoulder this time.

More lucidity floated back to me and past the constant hum of the box fan I'd set in the corner, I was able to make out a soft gurgling.

My lungs shut in a vice the moment my eyes opened.

Hovering over me was the strangest creature I'd ever

seen. Its skin was bumpy, similar to that of an octopus, with long tentacle arms that were devoid of suckers. At the ends of each of them—and there were too many to count—I saw the small wiggling forms of fingers. Two gently held my arm while one pressed over a small cut. Another, hovering in the air, held the baggie of crystals, and yet another, a knife from the kitchen.

My breathing hitched when I saw the slight discoloration on the tip.

Blood.

My blood.

Its swirling, purple eyes shot up to meet mine.

I screamed.

My throat went raw immediately, but I didn't stop, backpedaling off the bed, swatting at the millions—no, billions—of tiny, fleshy hands that reached for me. Eventually the mattress ended and I slammed against the floor.

The wind rushed out of me.

I couldn't breathe as that *thing* crawled over the bed, right towards me.

"Wait," it croaked, "Beatrice, wait."

Tears blurred my vision. My back hit the wall, right above me was the circular window that overlooked the front yard.

I didn't know if it could open, but I wasn't beyond breaking it.

A tentacle wrapped around my arm, slipping on the blood seeping from two thin slices. The pressure it exerted wasn't a lot, but it was enough to make me yelp with whatever air I could manage.

"Beatrice—"

Wheeling back a foot, I kicked wildly. No hits landed.

Instead, another tentacle wrapped around my limb, pinning it to the floor.

Whatever could be classified as this thing's face stretched towards me.

"My Researcher, breathe."

Against my better judgement, I stopped struggling.

Within those eyes, wide, multifaceted, swirling with purple energy and stars, there was something familiar.

Someone familiar.

"I'm sorry," it croaked. The voice was shattered, the breath rancid.

"What are you doing to me?" I choked out.

The creature spoke as if it knew me but I did not know it. In the back of my mind, a voice recognized it as the Traveler...but she was not this.

It shook its head. "It's...hard. To explain."

The knife rose again, and I thrashed. "No, you let me go!"

"Stop, Researcher, you're only making this worse."

My head began to swim. "Let me go!"

The thing's grip—*her* grip—began to slip. The blood, sweat, and whatever mucus this creature secreted to stay moist was enough to let me slip my arm out.

I knocked the knife aside, shoving past and trying to run for the stairs.

The tentacle around my leg tightened.

My body slammed against the floor, stars clouding my vision.

She stood before me, shimmering as always, hand outstretched.

"Beatrice." Her voice was low, stern.

Desperate.

"Listen to me."

Chapter SIXTEEN
white noise

FOR THE FIRST time, the void was not cradling me. The cosmos pressed in on all sides, cloudy nebulas and stars and solar systems circling my wrists, pressing against my cheeks, looping around my neck. The tiny bursts of heat from each star burned my skin.

She stood at a distance, hand still outstretched. Each step she took sent strange ripples across the plane of space she somehow managed to walk on. "Beatrice, listen to me."

Her words reached my ears but they meant nothing. There was no odd comfort in them anymore, no intrigue. The form that had held me against that wall raced through my mind, entirely at odds with the creature before me now. "What *are* you? Really?"

Wisps of starlight hair floated around her with each shake of the head. She came closer now, eyes wide and burning. "I told you, and I did not lie."

"A traveler. Yes. But what was...what was *that*?"

The comet-tails making up her lashes fluttered shut. She shook her head.

My throat constricted. "What do you *want* with me," I hissed.

"I did not *lie*," she repeated. Her eyes found mine, rage sparking for a mere moment. "You and I want the same things. To explore. To learn. *That's* why I came to you, that's why I found you. I..." a hand drifted close to my face.

Despite my attempt to throw my body away from her, I couldn't move.

Still, her hand paused, then drew back. "I was looking for you. Everyone else failed me, Beatrice. They all claimed they were perfect, that they were what I needed. But they weren't." A smile stretched across her face, gentle—were it not for the supernovas in her eyes. "You are."

I shook my head. One final attempt, violent and fearful, threw me free from the shackles of the universe. Pain bloomed along my shoulders, elbows, and hips as I rolled along the strange floor of wherever we were.

"Beatrice, listen to me!" Her shout tore through me like a shockwave. Glancing back, I watched ancient fury dissipate from her shoulders. With a deep breath, she stepped forward. Hands fitted themselves beneath my armpits and hoisted me to my feet so that we might stand opposite one another. "Please." Her hands slid down my arms, fingers weaving through mine. "Let me explain. Give me a chance to explain what's going on, fully."

For a moment, I almost thought she was human. The earnest fear and desperation in her eyes...I'd seen it before.

That look was never one I'd appreciated.

I shook my head, pulling my hands from hers.

Then, the humanity was gone. Suddenly there was no woman there, begging me to let her speak, to hear her out. There was something much more, much more volatile and unpredictable. Black holes appeared behind her eyes, supernovas flared along her collarbones. A vast, unforgiving, primordial darkness appeared in her features, and with it, awe bloomed within my chest.

A shuddering breath worked from my lips, eyes tracing hers. The Traveler remained unblinking. The white noise she carried with her grew, filling my mind, working to loosen my muscles.

I let it.

"Alright."

She nodded. "I never lied to you. I am a traveler, that's my...whole being. I am nothing if I do not explore. I am nothing if I do not learn."

Despite the panic still writhing within my chest, I couldn't help my gaze drifting over the entrancing void of space that made up her features.

"But I cannot do it alone," she whispered. "I was looking for someone to help me. And..." a smile flickered over her face, now inches from mine, "I found her." Her hands drifted up my arms again, pressing lightly on the bare expanse of my forearms and biceps.

Heat burned where, moments earlier, I'd been cut and bleeding.

"You'd asked what those crystals were before," she murmured. "And that's hard to explain. They're nothing like what you have here, they're...alive. In a way." Her head bobbed back and forth, "they get me where I need to go, but I can't talk to someone if they haven't...taken them."

"So you..."

She nodded, meeting my eyes once more. That featherlight touch drifted back down to my hands. "It's okay. There will be no adverse affects. There shouldn't be. It'll just be me, here. All the time."

Something tightened within my chest.

"I give you a gateway to exploration and you take me to explore. Right?"

Even as I nodded, the hair on the back of my neck stood up.

"I asked you if you wanted to see the universe the way I did, and you accepted." she said softly. "So let me."

The heat and deafening roar emanating from her form drew me in.

Who was I to say no to this? Whatever this was—mental break, psychosis, a really weird dream—it was everything I'd ever wanted.

Fuck the program, I was holding the hands of the cosmos itself. And she was asking me to go with her.

Still, that primal animal beat within the cage of my chest. *This is insane*, it cried, *you'll die.*

"What would we do?" I asked.

That too-wide smile reappeared. "We're going to drink diamond rain and walk on moons your kind haven't even discovered yet. We'll watch the dance of pulsars, the births of black holes—anything you could ever want to do, Researcher. Find a star no one has laid claim to and name it after yourself, if you wanted." Her hand rose slowly.

This time, I did not flinch away when it rested against my cheek.

Every flare from each star that made up the strange form of mass that was her hand sent a shiver down my spine.

"I will show you what you need to do to see it. My only ask is that you bring me with you as well."

Her white noise enveloped me, soft and gentle and eternal.

Even as waves of fear rippled through me, everything fell into place.

Space, the cosmos—that was where I belonged. Not in a lab.

It had always been trying to call me home. I just finally was able to hear it.

Chapter SEVENTEEN
just white noise.

A STIFF GASP invaded my lungs. My arms, from shoulder to fingertip, ached with the effort it took to push myself upright. Sitting back, the silence of the room enveloped me. The box fan in the corner had fallen silent. How long I'd been asleep, I didn't know, but I hadn't moved from where I'd fallen.

Something slimy drifted free of my leg.

Disgusted, desperate fear shot through me, the same way it does when weeds brush against your feet when swimming, and I yelped.

That image of the creature looming over me flashed through my mind again.

Whatever ambient noise the room offered was drowned out in the thunderous cacophony of my pulse in my ears once more. It did not go away as I peered at the fallen creature behind me, tentacles splayed in a coiled, knotted mass, slick in the blue light of morning with blood and other secretions.

How did I know this wouldn't kill me?

Beneath it, a disgusting greasy stain was already seeping into the rug beneath the bed.

Cheryl would be pissed, and I'd definitely have to pay a damages fee.

Using the railing for support, I pushed myself to my feet. My eyes passed over my arms in a cursory glance. Those cuts had already begun to heal. Blood mixed with whatever mucus the creature secreted to seal them formed those same thick, heavy scabs.

Just the lightest touch near the incision sites was enough to feel the sharp lump of crystal buried beneath my skin.

My breath hitched as I pressed.

It scraped against muscle, against tendon.

Nausea churned my stomach.

Too late to get them out now, even as my mind reeled once more with any and every cure for a splinter I'd ever been taught.

Stepping sideways to the lamp by my bedside, I flicked it on. Over the mattress I could only make out the general lump of the creature. As I walked back around, that nausea grew.

The closest thing I could equate it to was an octopus, but even that wasn't right. There had to be a body in there, somewhere—I'd seen a head, and face, but as I leaned down and rolled it over, the light from my lamp caught on the bits of flesh that stuck to the plush rug, the slatted wood floor. Decaying flesh stuck to my hands, slicking them with an acrid stench.

I stared at it for a long moment.

Then I moved.

• • •

THE walk through the woods was agonizing. One mile with a body on my back was much harder than it looked in the movies.

However this creature was built allowed for its tentacles to be entirely devoid of bones. With this unnerving discovery, I'd wrapped a few of them around my shoulders and waist and tied them in a knot. Thankfully, the decay seemed to act as a glue to hold the fleshy knot in place.

After a walk that had begun to seem too long, I began tripping over fallen logs and broken trees. Ahead, the crater was visible through the trees. A large outcropping of rock had already been painted pink by the sun filtering through the grey-blue clouds.

Around me, the remaining leaves shuddered on their branches.

It took work to untangle the ties I'd fastened for myself. Flesh tore. Melted. Stuck beneath my nails and caught in my throat with every breath. Eventually, though, the knot I'd tied around my shoulders broke free. Then, fingers broke off of the one around my waist as I tore that apart.

There was no use being ceremonious with it. Bending at the waist, I pulled it off my back over my shoulder. The weight of the alien nearly dragged me down the slope with it, but I managed to regain my footing and release my grip. Bits of flesh tore off on rocks—others stuck to the corpse.

It rolled to a stop in the middle of the crater, just feet from where its ship impacted days ago.

I stared at it, chewing on the side of my tongue.

I should have felt bad for it.

Here was this pilot, easily a couple thousand light years from home, dumped unceremoniously into a pit. Not even back with their ship, as any captain from Earth would have wanted. As any captain from earth *deserved*.

Yet, all I offered was a click of my tongue and a nod.

Trembling fingers dug the box of matches out of my pocket and struck one, flicking it down into the crater. It bounced off a rock a foot away.

I frowned, lit another, and chucked it a little harder.

This time it landed on an outstretched tentacle. Slowly, the flame grew, traveling up the appendage to the main body, engulfing the alien in an inferno.

If I couldn't give it it's ship, the least I could do was make sure whoever or whatever had the ship would never have the pilot.

She seemed pleased enough with that decision.

The sun began to break through the trees across the way. I sat down at the edge of the crater, fishing my phone from my pocket. It had charged enough overnight that I felt comfortable snagging it before carting this alien out here for a shitty approximation of a viking funeral.

I didn't question how I suddenly had cell service here.

With the surge of energy that passed along my bones, I knew well enough.

It took a moment to find her contact, dial it.

The buzz of a connecting call became hypnotic before it was broken by a cheery voicemail greeting clearly recorded a year or two ago.

"Hi Cheryl," I said, smiling out at the impact crater

and the burning corpse within it. It felt strange—forcing that telephone-smile, so she heard in my voice that I was okay.

Looking up from the body in the pit, I smiled wider.

My cheeks hurt.

"Sorry to call so early, I just...I think I need to cut my trip short. My whole plan with coming out here was to unwind and unplug from my program but...I think I just made a huge breakthrough with my thesis. Gimme a call back and we can work out payment before I go."

I ended the message and tucked my phone between the disturbed dirt beneath me and my thigh.

As the sun rose higher, the final stars, the brightest ones, started to blink out in the light sky. Crisp autumn air filled my lungs with each deep breath.

There was no birdsong.

Only white noise.

Acknowledgements

With a short novella comes short acknowledgements.

Thank you to everyone who got excited when I announced this.

Thank you to my husband, for checking on me in my favorite old writing chair with a "how's the writing going?" and a kiss on the cheek. Thank you for getting excited when I'd tell you the part I was working on. I love you more than anything.

Thank you to Abby and Arley, for being my two first friends who shared and encouraged my interest in the strange and unusual. I have a bigger project to honor you coming in the following years.

And thank you to anyone who has read this. I appreciate you more than you know.

Lila Samson is a Minnesota born-and-raised author and artist. Her works mainly focus in Fantasy or Science Fiction, though that's bound to change at some point.

She currently lives in Minnesota with her husband and their two cats. You can find her on TikTok at @lilasamsonauthor and on Instagram at @shelvedbylila.

www.ingramcontent.com/pod-product-compliance
Lightning Source LLC
Chambersburg PA
CBHW061548310726
48972CB00008B/2664